I0565481

THE BEGGAR'S COIN

SHIPWRECKT BOOKS PUBLISHING COMPANY
Up On Big Rock Poetry Series
Winona, Minnesota

Other books by Lee Henschel Jr.

Short Stories of Viet Nam

The Sailing Master Book One, Coming of Age

The Sailing Master Book Two: The Long Passage

The Sailing Master Book Three: Letter of Marque

The Sailing Master Book Four: Gods of Clay

THE BEGGAR'S COIN

SHORT STORIES OF VIETNAM & THE EPIC POEM, THE 'NAM

LEE HENSCHEL JR.

Cover and interior design by Shipwreckt Books.
Character image on front cover translates as, "Vietnam."
Author photo by Billie Barthelemy—Bird of Paradise Designs.

Shipwreckt Books Publishing Company
357 W. Wabasha Street
Winona, Minnesota 55987

Short Stories of Vietnam, originally published in 1981, is reprinted with
permission of the author.
Portions of the epic poem, "The 'Nam," previously appeared in *Lost Lake
Folk Opera - Black April Issue, 40 Years since the Fall of Saigon*, April 2015
V3- N1.

Library of Congress Control Number: 2023937884

Copyright, Lee Henschel Jr. 2023
Shipwreckt Books Publishing Company 2023
ISBN: 979-8-9875338-4-0

This book is dedicated to the children of Southeast Asia.

Table of Contents
Short Stories of Vietnam &
The 'Nam

People ask: "When were you in Vietnam?"
My answer: "Last night."

"... for the public, it seemed, preferred to believe that which disturbed it least, and to ignore the troublesome information. Which is a common failing of all nations."
—from "The Far Pavilions" by M.M. Kaye

Forward

A few years back, when I was a student teaching in public school, I read a letter to my seniors signed by President Nixon and was addressed to everyone who was graduating that spring, regardless of political beliefs, gender, age, or class rank. It was a democratic letter. My seniors, as I recall, weren't impressed; not much can impress seniors. But I remember a simile expressed in the letter signed by the President. He said that life was like a series of short stories. One story ends and another begins. On and on until the last page, and I guess that's not a half-bad way of looking at life.

Except for this: for some people, say dead GIs and civilians caught up in the Vietnam war, the story, their lives, ended before the last page was reached. Years from now the Vietnam war may have attained no more importance than perhaps the War of the Austrian Succession has for us today. There are, to my knowledge, no short stories of the Austrian Succession. Probably no one cares about the dead GIs and civilians of that time. But the lives lost in Vietnam mean plenty to us here, as we dash through the nineteen-eighties. Their short lives maybe were short stories but ending with no final straightening out of loose ends. But our lives, if we allow them, will turn into novels and, if we're lucky, perfect one-word poems. Life is like that, too.

First Day

you place yarrow sticks on the pyre,
and return the beggar's coin

It was somewhere over Mount Fuji when I finally got a hold of my thoughts and was able to put into words what was happening to me. I'll have to take this year in 'Nam one minute at a time, one day at a time. Forget about next year, or when you'll get out of here. Think about here and now because that's all there is. Mount Fuji, rising so grandly and symmetrically and out of the heart of Japan, has a way of clearing one's thoughts. It's been doing that for people for thousands of years.

Henry Browning was on a roll, now. It was something most veterans usually do from time to time. It's called "a flashback" in contemporary parlance. For Henry, this flashback had been sparked by his friend's son, Paul. He asked Henry what it was like over there and Henry had tried to keep his response clear and simple. And this, he knew, was a distortion, but what the hell, he thought, Paul's only ten. Still, ten is older now than when I was ten. Besides, the child is the father of the man, when it comes to the nature of things. It's ironic, Henry thought, that here's Paul, who wasn't even born when I was in 'Nam, asking me the questions that hardly anyone else even asked. Henry wondered why that was. He asked Paul why hardly anyone asked him about Vietnam.

Paul, ever thoughtful and deliberate in answering, replied that maybe no one really wanted to know. Henry said that he supposed Paul was right.

They watched the football game on television for a while longer and then Henry asked Paul why he wanted to know what others before him didn't care to know. Paul told him he was doing a report for his history class on American wars.

"Oh," Henry replied.

The game was over now, and a re-cap of world news took its place on the screen. Paul had fallen asleep, and so it was up to Henry to provide himself with the stuff of life until he, too, could fall asleep.

"A report for my history class," he mused softly aloud. And what was it like over there? He wondered. Sometimes I'm not so absolutely sure it ever happened, if I was ever there. Mount Fuji was so beautiful when we flew over it. The pilot flew over especially for us because we were a troop plane. Some of us had already been anointed with the invisible mark. Everybody is marked, Henry reminded himself. Everyone dies. But I hated that pilot for flying over Mount Fuji, as if some of us would never return, or never be able to look out a window again. It was a thoughtful enough gesture, he reminded himself, it's just that you hated everything at that point. Most of all you hated yourself.

He hated and was scared of the insecurity of the year ahead. He remembered the hundred stories. They were all told by service vets who had been tainted and hardened and demented or changed by the insecurity and the emotional vacuum. One career sergeant put it this way: "You get off the plane and they give you an M-16 and a machete and line you up and tell you to chop your way through the jungle and after a year they line you up again and take away your machete and your M-16 and tell you to get back on the plane."

No, it can't be that way, Henry had thought. That's too simple. He knew it was only the gallows humor of some guy who wanted to get a reaction.

This flashback was unfolding slowly, Henry knew, but it took its own course, making its own neurological connections with his subconscious, bringing the unrelated and meaningless vignettes of his past to the forefront.

He knew he would be landing in Cam Ranh Bay and he wondered how it was that a Vietnamese place could have such an American name. But then he saw it spelled out on his orders and saw the difference. It wasn't spelled Camron at all. It's all going to be different. And he landed in the dead of night while it was raining. The rain smelled the same as home. When he disembarked, he grabbed onto that similarity so that hopefully things could proceed in a logical order. But the air was thick and black, and he didn't know his directions. And he didn't know if the mama-sans and papa-sans who stood inside the terminal were the enemy. It didn't make any difference, though, because he was unarmed and green, like a bottle lamb for the butcher of God, the God that had nothing to do with Southeast Asia.

There was another bus ride and that's all the service really amounted to: one long bus ride. The bus driver was in the Air Force. He was unarmed, or so it looked, and relaxed, or so it seemed. Henry was tired, he recalled, and tried for some sleep. Eyes shut, bouncing along in the dark, he thought of absolutely nothing, but not for long.

Somewhere during Henry's bus ride, a sapper had infiltrated the main ammunition dump on the peninsula, Henry was to learn. The sapper carried thirty-five pounds of explosives and a detonator. He found the fifteen-hundred-pound bombs and used his satchel charge to set them all off which, in turn, set off most of the rest of the dump. All I wanted was some peace and quiet and what do I get?

The sky lit up. Henry, riding in a bus not very far from the ammunition dump, took his first look at Vietnam. The bus driver pulled off to the side of the road, took a pistol from the glove compartment, ran out and jumped in the ditch. A sergeant came up from the back of the bus and yelled at the driver to either get his ass back in and drive like hell to a cantonment area or he was going to drive himself. Then the concussion hit. It rocked the bus. Henry remembered wanting to do something. But what? I was never trained to ride in a bus while the world was blowing up. So he sat stark still. Maybe death would miss him if he sat still. Finally, the bus got rolling again. By this time traffic was heavy. Ambulances, jeeps, APCs, whatever, all headed for the dump. The bus driver delivered them. Everyone got out. Some guy pointed to a barracks for them to sleep in.

When the sun came up on Henry's first full day in Vietnam, his flash bulb vision of the terrain was confirmed. Cam Ranh Bay was a sandy, fly-blown weed-attached, huge redundancy of hills that surrounded an estuary. It's a big fucking ant hill, he thought, crawling with trucks, and jeeps and cars and Hondas and buses, plus ants, roaches, mosquitos and Americans and Vietnamese and, he was to find out later, Cambodians, Laotians and Indians. Henry knew his name, and his service number and what the rain had smelled like. He knew there had been huge explosions in the middle of the night. And he knew what his boots and his campaign togs felt like. These were his first impressions of Cam Ranh Bay, which wasn't at all like Camron.

By nine (0900) it was hot and sticky, and Henry didn't know anything more about Vietnam but at least he found a urinal, which, in those parts, was called a piss tube. It stank. A two-inch-long cock roach had drowned itself in urine. For decency's sake there were three walls around the piss tubes. Written on one of the walls was this:

> Read This—I spent my time in Vietnam and today I'm getting out of here. If you keep your mind on what you're doing, most likely you'll make it too. It'll change your life. I don't know anything anymore, except that I've been here a year and I made it and now I'm leaving. Most likely you won't die. You got to make up your mind right now that you'll make it.

Henry zipped himself up and backed out of the urinal. A long cock roach crawled up his leg. He shook it off and ground it into the red, wet sand. Paul, who was staying over for the evening, stirred sleepily in the big, living room chair. I wonder if Paul will ever have to fight a war. He remembered a conversation he heard between his father and a friend when he was only Paul's age. The only thing that really stuck in his mind was something toward the end.

"I'm not worried about you and me having another war," Henry's father's friend had said, "because we've already had ours. But I'm worried about him." He was pointing of course at Henry.

white gold

you ask no question
you question no answer
you die ten thousand times
not for the war lord, or the emperor, or a god
but for white gold on the coastal highway
a waist high drift spreading along the southbound lane
the rice harvest drying in the sun,
while your dalai lama, and your pope
wander the ruins of Con Ga
licking the wounds of the bullet pocked nave
their prayers, unvoiced in the moonlight
if not compassion, then kindness
if not kindness, then civility
if not civility, then white gold
you drop out of college with just one semester left
because you've been in school too long,
and are tired of it all
then, when you lose your 2-S Deferment,
the unseen hand draws the number seven for your
lottery ticket,
you get drafted and sent to the 'Nam,
to where you live and die inside the secret lie
except not the air,
for the air is on fire
you return home to write it
but you're not a writer, at least not yet,
and your words live dead until you understand,
and you begin to write inside the unseen
you wait in line
for fresh ODs, and a boonie hat
you stare at your new boots

ask why the helmet liner smells of sweat
ask how the dent in your steel pot got there
someone says shut up and keep moving
you pack your rucksack, just so
her last letter, ammo
C-rats, ammo
cigarettes, ammo
lighter fluid, ammo
bug juice, ammo,
more ammo
you sign for your M-16,
don't ask about the KIA tag on the muzzle
or the dried blood on the charging handle
you are not here to be brave
not here because it's right
or because it's wrong
not here to bleed or die
or to shed false light
you are here because you were afraid to say no
afraid to go to jail, afraid to run and hide in Canada
here because there's one thing for which you hunger
to smoke it, to snort it, to shoot it,
to become lost in it, never to be found
there it is, the unspoken truth

The Game

"I don't know if I can trust Jellicoe, sir. He's a horse shit shot." Sergeant Eckert, who was chief of smoke of a light artillery battery in the Americal Division, was explaining the situation to Captain Ventris, his commanding officer. "He's just a long drink of water. Not enough substance, if you know what I mean, sir, for this sort of thing."

"How is it that you know he can't shoot, sergeant? He's only been in this unit for a week." Captain Ventris had only been in the country for three weeks himself and knew through instinct and instruction to listen to NCOs such as Eckert when it came to matters concerning who to take on what patrols. The sergeant, a wily, black career man, was rounding off his third tour in Vietnam. This would be his last patrol. Most men in the gun sections knew him as the Oddsmaker. Sergeant Eckert, through his years of living in the South, through marriage to one woman for over twenty years, having raised a son and a daughter, through many things, had reduced life down to a set of very specific responses.

"I hates to play all them silly games," Eckert would relate on his rare, therefore genuine, evenings of lucid philosophizing. "There's only one Game. We all gots to play that Game so it's best to concentrate. You gots to commit to memory all the responses there is. Oh yeah! It's sort of like learning a special sort of multiplication table." Then he'd look around at his men, both black and white, and Mexican, too. "Now listen," he'd go on. "That's the easy part. Anyone can memorize, 'less he ain't got both oars in the water. You can always check to see how your memory's doin'. That's the part you can talk about and plan. It's the timing that's crucial, don't you see? Any fool can respond. Hell, I just told you that's what life is, just a bunch of responses to little games. But you gots to time your responses to coincide with what's happenin' in the big Game. Yeah, any fool can respond to little games, but a winner's the one that times hisself to the real Game. It's a matter of experience, and concentration. And luck."

The Game, at least another Vietnam chapter, was coming full circle for Eckert. In Eckert's mind, this was the period in which luck played a major role. His experience had taught him to concentrate on luck. Reduce the odds and try to live right. Eckert was trying to reduce the odds by taking Jellicoe off the patrol.

"Captain Ventris, I know he can't shoot 'cause of what I saw yesterday."

The captain asked what he saw.

"I told Jellicoe to hook up the Claymore mines out around the perimeter. I told him to make sure no one turned 'em in toward the firebase. I seen that happen once and . . ."

"Go on, sergeant. I know that trick."

"Yes, sir. Anyway, Jellicoe took his M-16 along with him and started working his way through the concertina. He looked all right so I went about my business."

Captain Ventris tried to listen to Sergeant Eckert but his mind kept switching channels. His mind wanted him to dwell upon the patrol that he and the sergeant were about to conduct. They were headed twelve kilometers out into the heart of the bush. Their coordinates were set, down to within ten square meters that surrounded a bunker. The bunker had been their target for the night before; a twenty-five-round mission. Only twenty-four of the rounds detonated.

"Well," Sergeant Eckert was saying, "about ten minutes later I hear an M-16 go off somewhere within the perimeter. I run out to the berm line and I see Jellicoe backing up. He'd stop and fire his rifle at the ground fifty feet in front of 'em. Then he'd back up some more and he could only move forward or backward 'cause he was hemmed in by the concertina. So I run over by him not really knowin' what to expect."

It was the captain's real first experience in the bush. He could have given it to Lieutenant Axelrod, his executive officer, by rights, but that was not his fashion.

"What was he shooting at, sergeant?" The captain asked.

The sergeant pulled up short in his conversation.

"It was a viper, sir. A two-step viper."

"Oh, I see," said Captain Ventris. "Did he hit the damn thing?"

"That's the problem, sir. He shot about a dozen time at it but it kept closing on 'em. The near misses just upset the damn thing more and more."

The captain wondered if they might encounter any two-step vipers out on patrol. The two-step, he recalled, was a viper whose poison attacked the nervous system. If one nailed you, you could take about two steps before you were dead.

Sergeant Eckert, apparently not hearing the captain's last question, or ignoring it, was gearing up for a full description of the two steps.

"These snakes is about two, two-and-a-half feet long, 'least the ones I seen. They's silver. A real tiny head, too, and a tail end that tapers off from 'bout the middle. But the really interesting thing 'bout them is . . ."

"So did Jellico ever hit this two-step?"

Sergeant Eckert, a little miffed at having his interesting part interrupted, switched back to Jellicoe.

"Well, by this time I was about twenty meters from 'em, on the inside of the wire, and I told him to put his rifle on automatic. I could tell he was nervous, and I guess I don't blame him. Anyway, he flips it on full auto and empties the magazine. Dirt flew up all over, but the snake keeps on 'a comin'. I told him to put in another clip and he looks at me surprised like, as if he wouldn't have thought of that on his own."

The NVA, thought Captain Ventris, if they were still around last night, surely heard that round go in that didn't detonate. They know we'll be searching for it. If we just let it go they could recover it for their own use. If we go after it, they know it will be today. They'll know when and where. He tried to tune in Sergeant Eckert.

"So he locks and loads and blows off another nineteen rounds but the snake, he keeps on comin'. Jellicoe, he whimpers a little, then turns around and starts runnin'. I yelled for him to load up again, but he looks at me again like I've seen guys look before. He ain't got no more ammo."

So Jellico chokes in a hot spot, Captain Ventris thought to himself. Or is that fair to say? It could have happened to anyone. Eckert doesn't want him though. Maybe it's because Jellicoe's shook up now and would be too jumpy.

"And you think, Sergeant Eckert, that Jellicoe shouldn't go on this mission because he can't shoot or because he choked?"

"Any way you want to put it, sir. I mean, maybe he choked 'cause he couldn't shoot, or maybe he couldn't shoot 'cause he choked. It don't matter. What matters is that that snake kept on comin' and someone else had to do it in."

"So what did happen, sergeant?"

"You won't believe this, sir, but that little Mexican guy, Ruiz? He's the one who keeps hollerin' 'bout how great he is at baseball and 'Nam's ruining his major league chances."

"Yes, Ruiz. I know him."

"Well, by now Riuz and 'bout half the firing battery are all standin' along the wire and Ruiz, he picks up this stone that's about the size of a goddamn baseball. He sort of winds up and pitches it at the snake that's after Jellicoe.

And he hits the stupid thing dead center and splits it in two like a piece of spaghetti. I couldn't believe it."

This is a hell of a war, Captain Ventris thought.

"Everybody's cheerin' Ruiz, slappin' him on the back, and saying he's got a great future in baseball when he gets back to the World. And Ruiz, he's eatin' it all up and tellin' everyone he ain't no bullshitter. They all go to the perimeter to check out the snake. All except Jellicoe. He's walkin' back to his section, real slow like. I tell him it's all right, just take it easy for a while and I'll get someone else to finish off the Claymores."

A small thought came to Captain Ventris.

"Why not replace Jellicoe with Ruiz for this patrol, Sergeant Eckert?"

"That's a good ida, sir, 'cept for one thing."

"What's that?"

"Ruis left this morning for Da Nang."

"What for?

"Some major league ball players are in Da Nang for the troops. Ruis wanted to go there to get some autographs."

"Hell of a war." Captain Ventris mumbled, mostly to himself.

"There it is, sir. There it is." Sergeant Eckert replied.

the unseen keep you awake
your night measured by smells
the Chanel No. 5, the amatol
you forget entire days, you forget entire lives
only you skin knows how long you've been here
gray dawn, mist in the valley
women singing,
you live separate lives, you lose them inside
your watch self winds, it glows in the dark
and the ones you love, will they understand?
satellites blink across the night sky, weeping
while you live inside the secret lie
for ten thousand years you deny your past
now you deny your future
you place yarrow sticks on the pyre,
returns the beggar's coin
and pray the moment will linger
will rise in the shimmering heat
lost now in the storm of maya
each morning the monks collects alms
women sing in the blue jungle,
and stop where the ancient spirts dwell
to ring a tiny bell

bayonet

your drill sergeant screams his command
tell me the spirit of the bayonet
To kill! To kill!
he fixes a bayonet on his M-16
and drives the rifle like a spear into a wooden plank
where it stands upright, muzzle down, quivering
he rips open his shirt
his black chest sweating in the Carolina sun
his keloid scars stand out pink
"I took these for my squad at A Shau.
Now you're my squad.
Do what I say, and you might live."

The Reb

Duke, who later asked us to call him the Reb, claimed that at one time in his military career he was a sergeant. No one in our squad believed him though, not because he was incapable of being a sergeant, but because we had all grown accustomed to his tall tales. This, we figured, was just another tall tale.

He and I were friends, maybe because I had what he referred to as a southern name. The Reb was from Tennessee and he had a great faith in the second coming of the south, which, I deduced, would occur shortly before or after the second coming of the Lord. Maybe we were friends because I rarely accused him of telling tall tales. I enjoyed his stories almost as much as he did, and usually had no comment with anything more than an expletive in it here or there, or perhaps a question, either to clarify a hazy point or just to get him back on track. I liked him because, well, just because, I guess.

He was the friendly sort, and of the typical, at least to me, "Johnny Reb" build. Let's say six feet tall with a wiry frame held together with long, sinewy muscles, stylized by somewhat of a beer gut. His face of juts and crags was an out-of-doors variety, with a protruding chin, definite cheekbones, (Duke claimed Cherokee blood) still, blue eyes and black, wavy hair. He could have had a full, black beard if he didn't shave. Every now and then, when he got drunk, he would rub the striker of his Zippo lighter up and down his forearms, setting his heavily thatched hair on fire. Then he would howl with a bawdy, resonating tone. And of course Duke had his Tennessee drawl which, as he loved to boast, was of the Memphis extraction. Memphis, for Duke, was more than an explanation for the universe; it was the universe. Everything else was merely unfinished business set adrift in some sort of holding pattern, waiting to be digested by the Memphis point of view. I guess Duke and I were friends because I knew

Memphis, having worked there several times, and could talk to him about Elvis Presley. He was his living idol. Duke claimed proud ownership (back in the World) of every last Presley album, plus a memorabilia collection that was second to none. He even had a satellite collection of taped albums in 'Nam that he faithfully carried with him.

Our friendship was sealed on the night I helped him record an Elvis Presley marathon broadcasted over Armed Forces Radio. The recording session, upon recollection, was a microcosm of Duke's experience in 'Nam. We had nothing fancy for recording. We couldn't "patch in," as the saying goes, so we had to record over the air. This meant that any background noise would be recorded along with "Jail House Rock" and other such hits. At the time, we were camped in relative splendor inside the perimeter of a heavy artillery unit. We were on unofficial stand down, with nothing better to do than loll the night away by listening to the radio. But the artillery unit had a busy night, with each of the four guns taking turns shooting an all-night harassment and interdiction mission. Our luck determined that whenever Elvis began to sing, the fire mission would start up. If we quit recording, then the fire mission would cease. At first Duke and I took it all in stride, with no overt attitude concerning fate, but as the hours passed, it seemed that there was some sort of conspiracy between the love of his life and explosions.

As it ended up, Duke recorded four hours of Elvis. Each song contained about two or three reports from the heavy artillery unit in the background. Duke and I spent about ten months together and every time he played those tapes we shared a private laugh.

Even though I doubted some of his stories I rarely rebuked him. I never really cared about their validity, but one evening I called him. We had just returned from the field. Duke's right hand was taped up in gauze from a trip flare burn. We had been setting out flares, working as a team, when I realized he was taking unnecessary chances with a primed flare. He was trusting the loose trip wire to hold down the pin instead of holding it in his hand. I got my hands out of the way, told him what he was doing and then walked away. In about thirty seconds I heard the flare go off and I turned to see Duke rolling around on the ground holding his hand. He had a large, second-degree white phosphorous burn across the palm of his hand; good for some time off.

We sat there drinking some beer and sharing a bowl of marijuana. I asked him why he did it.

"Wall, I jes' dun'no, Clay. I reckon I wan'ed some tam ouf. 'Sads, t'aint nuthin' c'mparred ta ween I wuz in Hail's Angels."

"Oh?" I asked. "You were in Hell's Angels?"

"Yep." He geared up, readying himself to tell me all about his experiences with the Angels. I had always been interested in the Hell's Angels since, back in the World, I had crossed paths with a group trying to live like the Angels did. I was playing in a rock band in California when we were asked to do a gig for a biker party. To make a long story short, these folks had all the trappings, right down to some really nice Harleys. They had the beer and the whiskey and the downers and the pot. They had the obligatory Harley which had been driven through the front door and into the living room. Some girl was pulling train, which is to say she was spreading her legs for all the guys at the party. Luckily, I was just a musician, so I didn't count. They had one really drunk guy who, at about three in the morning, pulled out his .38 Police Special and tried to keep the band from leaving. And they had an older dude, who sat cross-legged on his old Harley out in front rolling a cigarette.

"Put the gun away, Donny," the older guy said to the drunk. "The band's tired. They played for six hours. Let 'em go."

Well, Donny put away his .38 and let us go. These guys even had the police surrounding them, out there in the Sacramento suburbs, letting people out of the area but not letting anyone in.

Duke told me how it was with the Angels and him. I asked him how he got in and he told me about his initiation. It seems he had to bring along a girl who would pull train.

"I don't know, Duke," I told him. "Somehow you just don't seem to have that temperament."

But Duke went on to explain how he had to run the gauntlet.

"I had to fa'ht ever wun of 'em. 'un they was armed lak woun'n b'lieve."

"Armed, were they?" I asked.

"Yep," Duke explained. It seemed that he had to prove how tough he was by fighting every one of them.

I asked how he did. That's when he pulled out his Zippo and set his forearm ablaze. He gave his "Johnny Reb" war hoop. I guess I was to assume that that was the answer to how he did.

"What else did you have to do, Duke?"

"Beaucoup drugs, Clay. Mucho."

"How much?"

That's when it started. Afterward I told myself that I should have known that I should have been on the lookout. Duke went crazy every once in a while. Burning himself with the trip flare was a sign. So was the trick with the Zippo. They were signs of a tendency toward self-destruction.

We were sitting by a beer cooler. A boy-san had just sold us a case of black-market beer. The plan was to share it with the squad, but it didn't work out that way. Duke gave me the Vietnam stare, then he reached in the cooler, pulled out a beer, popped the top and chugged it. Then another. And another. He chugged ten beers in a row. I also had bought a gram of heroin from the boy-san. Duke took it out of my pocket, cracked the vial, poured half the powder into the cap of the vial and snorted it. He set it aside and chugged four more beers. Then he snorted the other half of the vial, threw it away and went for another can of beer.

I was getting worried by now. When was he going to stop? I knew what he was doing. He was proving to me that he was in the Hell's Angels. He didn't think I believed him. But he could die if he didn't stop. But Duke was a proud man. To stop him in, in his condition, would have meant a lot of kicking and gouging and rolling around in the dirt. I was ready to do it, though, because he was killing himself. But halfway through his fifteenth beer Duke went over backward and passed out.

There was only one thing for me to do. I had to get him to his rack and stay with him, so he didn't throw up on himself and suffocate. I dragged him into the hootch and laid him on his stomach with his head over the edge of the rack. He didn't move. I smoked a few more bowls of marijuana and then stretched out on the floor next to Duke. I told myself never to call him on a story again. Never, even if they were tall tales.

knowing

you arrive in the 'Nam not knowing
not knowing how long they are
or how they slide over your boot
not knowing they eat dead meat
not until you watch centipedes on the jungle floor
not knowing the banded krait is slow and lethargic
or that it buries its head in its coil when provoked
or why it's called the two-step viper
not knowing, until night falls

night

you feel it all day
not speaking, never thinking
you wait for the women singing
for the wind in the bamboo
for the drone of the sea,
and the Na River
you wait for the dream that will come at the end
and later, at the beginning

dawn

full moon pulling the tide off shore
rinsing last night's blood from the 'Nam

the slow waltz

02:00 hours
you know what the flame will draw,
and you won't light it
not now, not in this dark hour
not when the Cong watch for it
not when the others depend on you for their sleep,
if not their rest
save it for another time, another place
the slow waltz of candlelight
a form of prayer

mantra

a Vedic litany resonates in the abandoned stupas
there it is, there it is
it don't mean nothin'
it don't mean nothin'

The 5:30 News

When we finally returned to base camp from a forty-day hip shoot we all had plenty of money and a few days off in which to spend it. My friend Patty, who we called Gulch for some unexplained reason, found a portable television in the village for a hundred dollars. As Gulch stood in the open market among the ducks, lanterns and Indian silver traders bickering with the old mama-san over the price of the television, the thought occurred to me, for I was acting as Gulch's second, so to speak, that there was not a great deal of common sense involved in this sort of trade. I realized, however, that it would be next to impossible to try to talk Gulch out of what he wanted. Besides, I suspect that the mama-san with whom Gulch was dealing could read my face, as well as Gulch's, and would have shut me up quickly if I had the notion to dissuade my friend.

We would be going into the field again soon, I believed, and this would necessitate the leaving behind of most bulky or impractical objects. But to remind Gulch of this pending reality would do no good, for I could see that he was bent on having the set and the mama-san was fast closing the deal. Before I knew it, Gulch and I were strolling down the shade boulevard of the main street with television in hand, looking for a cruising Lambretta to taxi us back to our base camp on the outskirts of town. The expression on Gulch's face indicated the joy experienced in perhaps finding a rare artifact, or maybe returning home with a trophy. I felt that his common sense, what little of it he had, finally had deserted him. But then, Gulch had chosen a route in his way of handling things that none of us had ever tried. After spending six of his twelve months in Vietnam, he had elected to return home; back to the World, as we called it. Most of us, when it came our turn to leave, went to Hong Kong, or Taiwan, or maybe even Hawaii, but never back to the World.

That, in the minds of most soldiers I knew, would have been too great a risk. Suppose you didn't feel up to coming back to the war? Suppose nobody understood you back home? What if your fine edge of awareness could not be re-honed? Besides, why not see some of these East Asian circumstances while you had the chance? None of us wanted to go home only to have to return, none of us except Gulch, who returned all the way to Indiana to see family and friends and his hometown. And it was shortly after he return to Vietnam that he acquired the television.

As things worked out, we were assigned to a new firebase on the same afternoon Gulch bought his television. I laughed at first, thinking we would have to part with it, but we found out our new firebase was set up on the inland side of Cam Ranh Bay, just a few miles from our base camp. Gulch could bring along his television, much to the pleasure of our gun section, excluding me. I hated television. I don't know why, and I could never explain to Gulch why it was that I rarely visited him after he bought the set. I guess you could call it wave confusion; I could not accept the contradictory messages sent forth in and by television. What one saw and heard on television contradicted with what one felt and thought in the field, obviously, and the following surrealism resulted in some sort of mental indigestion. I wanted Gulch to leave the television at base camp.

"Leave it, Gulch, we won't have any electricity where we're headed."

"Of course we will, Billy," Gulch replied, quite correctly.

"There won't be any good programs on," I insisted.

"Sure there will be! The World Series starts next week." He reminded me."

"Baseball sucks. I hate television. Please leave it behind. Sell it. You can sell it for more than you bought it for."

"But Billy, what's wrong with a little television once in a while?" Gulch asked.

"I don't know. It's just not right, I guess. The people back home, like the folks you just got done visiting, they think we're all over here dying 'cause of what they hear on the news. And here we are watching fucking Captain Kangaroo."

"Hey, come on Billy. Captain Kangaroo's never been on over here and you know it."

"What's the difference?" I asked. "It's all a matter of watching television in a combat zone. You know what I mean?"

Gulch lit a cigarette. "This isn't really a combat zone."

I reminded him that we were heading for one in a few days.

"Just forget it, Billy. I'm takin' the TV. You don't have to watch." He turned his back and began tuning his set.

I decided to change my tactics. I can't say when I actually decided to get rid of the television, but when Gulch turned his back, I knew something would have to happen. I'm not stupid. I can calculate and conspire. Usually, I get what I want if I plan things well enough and I'm patient. Gulch was, in my estimation, young and tender, susceptible to manipulation and unaware of subterfuge. Several days went by. We convoyed for two days, moving our guns, ammunition, supplies and communications to the foot of some unnamed hill. Gulch and I were too busy to argue about his television. I treated him well and I believed in my sincerity. After all, Gulch and I were good friends and it's necessary to share hard work, food and stories. I almost felt like forgetting my plan. But one evening after mess I brought up the subject of the television as we sat watching From Here to Eternity on his, and the only set in the artillery.

"You know, Gulch," I began, "you paid for this set but everyone spends their free time watching it. You should charge for the privilege, or sell shares in its ownership, or maybe let someone else buy it for a while, like me, maybe."

Gulch sat forward, giving me a look of curious amazement.

"I though you hated television, Billy." Then he asked, "Why would you offer to buy this thing?"

I was prepared for this.

"Well," I said, "I changed my mind a little bit. I mean, I can't say I really dig TV, but as long as it's here, we might as well all enjoy it."

Timing, as it has been forever and, in all things, is crucial. I knew that if I acted quickly with Gulch that my chances of success would be better. I pulled out a wad of military pay certificates and plopped them on Gulch's lap.

"Here's a hundred bucks. Let me take the set for a while." Then I gave him the kicker. "If you want, you can retain the option of buying it back in a week."

Gulch cleared his throat, rubbed his eyes with his hands and then stared at me for what seemed a long time. Then he spoke.

"Billy? If I know anything about you at all, and maybe I don't, my guess is that you're fucking with me. I don't know what this is all about, but I really don't want to sell this TV, and especially not to you. You're liable to fuck it up right in front of me just for the hell of it. It's not like I can't get along without this thing, maybe I'll even get tired of it, but it's just my bag right now. Can you dig it? Some dudes drink, some smoke, some have girlfriends. I watch television. What's wrong with that?"

I shrugged it off.

"I mean, you're cool, Billy. You're good at what you do, but you're also a little bit crazy in the head. You're going home pretty soon, and not a bit too early, so just hold on for a while."

Gulch tossed the money back to me and excused himself. I sat there in front of the television, knowing that he had seen through me. Either Gulch was growing up, which, when I was to think back on it, was obvious, or I had failed to see my own obviousness or simplicity. His last few words ran through my mind. "You're going home soon and not a bit too early."

Well? I asked myself. Why not just go ahead with your plan? Just leave the money and take the set. I sat there for a moment thinking it over. Then I got up, pulled the plug on the set, took it off the ammunition box where it sat and put the hundred dollars in its place.

It was dark but I knew where I was headed; out to the gun pit where our eight-inch self-propelled howitzer sulked. No one saw me. No one was there as I placed the television in front of the track. I hopped in the driver's seat, flipped the ignition and started the diesel that drove the unit. It didn't take long for me to roll it forward, flattening the television. I swiveled on the crumpled mess just to make sure, just to stress a point, I guess. By the time I turned the motor off and climbed out our entire crew was in the pit, wondering if there was a fire mission or some other reason for the howitzer to be moved. They saw me. Then they saw the flattened television under the track and understood. Gulch stepped from the small crowd to inspect the thousands of crushed pieces spread out on the floor of the pit. He held his money in his hand.

I stood facing them all, half in defiance, half in guilt. It was a long time before anybody said anything. Finally, Gulch laughed. I was glad, but then, what else could he do?

the 5:30 news reveals
but it does not smell the blood
the words record,
but fail to account for the ones left burning
but the black and white stills,
they linger
you turn and search for the HUEY thumping the air
there . . . that black dot floating in the gray sky
squelch, radio talk, smoke marker
the HUEY lands on Hill 1113
you haul aboard, and the door gunner nods to the pilot
you lift off and climb out of range of small arms fire
the hill falls away
this hill is not a highland elephant lying on her side and
giving birth
these tall pines are not giraffes standing sentry on the
ridge line
but, in black and white stills they look that way
and that unfiltered light shining on you face,
a face you no longer know,
with eyes that see forward and back
seeing another time.

liberty dollar

your stomach turns
your bones ache
it hurts to move
you need another fix
and you're broke
except for your Liberty Dollar
brought to the 'Nam for good luck
but now you sell it for five bucks, MPC
and you snort the next vial of smack
you feel good
there it is, and it don't mean nuthin'
not until your stomach turns
and your bones ache

ho chi minh trail

by day,
the red mud caked on the feet of the buffalo boy
at night, the water buffalo stirs in his sleep
the Annamite Range looms unseen, and the Na River
runs silent
indifferent to the NVA, whose soldiers wheel bicycles
burdened with ammo, with rice, with medicine
and with letters from home
the fire mission begins, and the NVA units go to ground
and in the next valley, a regiment stops on the trail
listening, before moving on

very morning, just before third watch ended, she would come meandering out from the outskirts of Son Mao, a small hamlet on the costal plane. But actually, before you would ever see her, her arrival would be announced by the tinkling of tiny bells that were worn by her nanny goats. First the lead goat, a white, black and brown milk goat with an insane expression in her eyes would come down the path. She was usually followed by two or three yearling does. Inevitably, the old mama-san would bring up the rear, keeping order to the ritual. There was a sparse bit of open graze that she had picked out for her goats, and every day, unless it was raining, or unless it was forbidden by the military, you could depend on her and her goats spending a good part of the day out there.

She was an old mama-san. By looks she seemed at least in her eighties. A woman like here, though, is deceiving. She might have been much younger, or older. One red-caked tooth hung in her puckered, dry mouth. Her bewhiskered face wore the erosions of countless military crimes. You wouldn't think that she had any hair, but it was impossible to tell because of her obsequious conical hat. Her hands, like her face, portrayed a life that was born old. They protruded from the sleeves of a white shirt that she always wore. She washed her shirt every Tuesday in a little stream that ran next to the grass in the goat's graze, unless, of course, it was raining or the military forbade it. Her pants were of the pajama type, silk or more likely satin, a dusty and worn out black, and loose, even at her gaunt waist. She used some twine or an old shoelace to hold them on. She used her pants in various ways. She might wipe her face or nose on them, or her hands. She rolled them up as shorts, on occasion, to expose the knobby, age-darkened sticks that were her legs. She would wash her pants once a week too, on Thursdays, and put them on wet. In Song Mao nothing stayed wet for more than fifteen minutes unless it was the rainy season. Then things stayed wet for three months running.

Mama-san was just called mama-san. If you happened to meet her along the path or visited the stream during the day you might catch the bright flash of her eyes staring at you from under her hat. But she was not, as was the case with many like her, in good health. The poor are not healthy in a war zone. She smoked a nameless brand of cigarette, pre-rolled and the size and shape of a Camel. She would carry these in a bundle held together by a rubber band, or a string. It seemed there were a hundred to a bundle. Mama-san coughed in a consumptive, rattling manner. Sometimes she would hawk up some mucous-like glob after a long coughing spell. She would spit it out in front of her where it would dry in the sun as the flies feasted on it. Mama-san also partook in the habit of betel nut chewing. This was why her one remaining tooth was red. A betel nut is red and one who chews betel nut produces blood-red saliva. Usually mama-san's chin carried a thin stream of blood-red saliva from her mouth to a droplet that hung from her oval face. Many GIs believed she bled from the mouth. It drove the good-hearted ones a bit crazy.

Ferguson was a good-hearted GI. He was in our gun section where he fused projectiles for high explosives, beehive and white phosphorous rounds that we shot over mama-san's head on occasion. It bothered him to see her out there, so helpless and vulnerable and old. But Fergy, which is what we called him, was disturbed by more than mama-san's lack of safety. Fergy was bothered by the haunting suspicion that military service was rendering him insane. He said that mama-san's white and black and brown goat's eyes were a mirror of his own, that he would feel inside himself that he was slowly losing his marbles and that he had to get out of Vietnam. At first, after such statements, the members of our section would shake his hand in a fraternal way. But then a few months passed and Fergy began to discuss certain forms of behavior that he believed might clarify his dilemma to others. Shooting oneself was always a possibility, but it would have to be a perfectly placed shot. Otherwise, you're dead, or not too bad off. Anything in between was considered, by the authorities, as willful and beyond the ability of the insane. Shooing someone else was almost always considered aggressive and criminal unless, of course, it was the enemy. Not eating was considered a good deal for the cooks and drinking oneself to death or abusing some other drug was actually not very abnormal at all. Refusing to obey orders brought attention and one might be considered crazy for this, but only for not obeying orders. Running away was AWOL or, if serious enough, desertion.

Fergy's overwhelming compulsion, then, concerned finding the appropriate behavior to illuminate his loss of right reason. As time passed, Fergy could be found, more often than not, visiting the old mama-san. She knew no English, or at least she would not speak it or let on that she knew any. Fergy knew no Vietnamese. It was obvious, however, that he wanted to communicate with her. One may always depend on the youth of a nation to fill in such a gap. And so it was for Fergy. Many young men and women, and even more so, boys and girls, at that time in Vietnam, knew quite enough English to conduct business. The old mama-san kept a granddaughter, perhaps it was her great granddaughter, with her at most times. Lon was her name, as Fergy knew, for she supplied the enlisted men with little frozen bananas and even nice, round watermelons once in a while. For five dollars Fergy could speak to mama-san through Lon.

Mama-san fit into his plans. He had quite meticulously planned to be seen with mama-san. He wanted the more ranking members of the gun battery, such as the first sergeant, the executive officer, and the battery commander to wonder about all this. He succeeded admirably with all this, for on more than one occasion all three of them would stand on the berm line observing, through a shared set of field glasses, Fergy, Lon and the mama-san, who, in their own cozy group, relaxed by the stream, nestled in among the grazing nannies.

This routine went on for weeks, perhaps twice a week, until one day, at noon, Fergy wandered in through the front gate followed by mama-san, the white, black and brown nanny, (who had to be coaxed with a bit of banana) the doelings and Lon. Most of Fergy's friends, by this time, knew what he had in mind, and therefore were not surprised to see him stop in front of the first sergeant's hootch. He knocked. Because it was noon, he was sure to find he first sergeant in, lying with his hootch maid. Everyone knew it was crazy to disturb the first sergeant during lunch. Fergy knocked again. The door finally opened a crack. When the first sergeant's hootch maid, who was not dumb, analyzed the situation, she summoned the first sergeant.

He opened the door wide, standing in the shade of the eave, belly protruding over his olive drab shorts and t-shirt. The first sergeant was not one to stand on formality. The noon sun beat down on Fergy, mama-san, Lon and the goats. Those in the battery who were watching looked on in quiet expectation, and with a certain sort of respect for Fergy and his small entourage. Everyone knew that the first sergeant was an unforgiving bastard and that Fergy was out on a limb.

The first to break the silence was the lead nanny, who bleated out her displeasure. She was not pleased with the heat or the smell of the Americans and their firebase. As if this was his cue, the first sergeant cleared his throat and asked the obvious question.

"Just what the fuck do you think you're doin', Ferguson?"

Fergy was about to answer but the first sergeant spoke again.

"You know I'm not to be disturbed during lunch if we're not in the field."

"Yes, Top," Fergy started in, "But this is important."

He turned sideways to afford a better view of his little group.

"I," Fergy hesitated, "I want you to meet my future bride and her granddaughter. And her goats."

The first sergeant snorted. His hootch maid issued a derisive chortle.

"I'm in love with mama-san. She, she wants to come to America, back to the World. She's read a lot about it. I'm going to adopt Lon and I need for you to get all the paperwork going on this. I only have four months left in-country and I know it takes a long time so I . . ."

"Are you out of your fuckin' mind, Ferguson? She's," here the first sergeant pointed at mama-san, "ugly! And she's old enough to be King Tut's mother."

He was getting up a head of steam but then he stopped, reassessing the situation.

"Wait a minute, Ferguson. Ain't you the guy who keeps trying to prove how crazy he is?"

Fergy wagged his head back and forth.

"You must be thinking of someone else, Top. You see, mama-san means a lot to me. I worry about her when we shoot over her head. She doesn't understand any of this. But if I could just . . ."

"Ferguson!" The first sergeant was yelling. "I'll tell you what I'm gonna do for you 'cause I'm such a nice guy. You're gonna get that mama-san and that kid and those fucking goats the fuck off this firebase and never, ever are you gonna pull any shit like this again. Is that clear to you, Ferguson? Is it?"

Fergy, who was standing at a relaxed sort of self-appointed attention, screamed out, "Yes, sir!"

Then he saluted, which was a taboo, performed a ragtag about face and herded his little family out the gate and down the path. The first sergeant stood in the shade inside his door. His face and arms exhibited a brilliant, high blood pressure, red. He smoked and glowered. Finally he withdrew, slamming shut his door.

We thought we had just witnessed the end of another episode in Fergy's search for deliverance. All things must pass. But some things, however, do not pass so easily.

The next day, at ten past noon, Fergy wandered slowly into the firebase, heading toward the first sergeant's hootch. Behind him followed mama-san, her goats, and Lon.

the light in this valley, you've seen it before
but not just as light
you've seen the enemy, and he isn't you
he's not the one standing in the stream
or the one no one sees but you
and the feel of this place, you've felt it before
but only as the last thing remaining
before the light turns pale
and the sound,
you've heard it before

the rocks in this stream do not wait

you stand on the path
they stream by you
they flow around you
they move through you
because you're the unseen
the invisible, and the untouched
but then you feel his stare, and turn to face him
he watches you, unsure of who you are
you ask why he,
why he alone within this flow
why he senses you
you ask if he feels the rhythm of your poem
if he hears the unspoken rhyme
he says you are dead
not dead, but in another place
in the blue jungle
where ancient spirits dwell
where all poets arrive in honor
where every poem in cherished
he tells you to move on
for the rocks in this stream do not wait

white dahlia

you do not stand before the wall
you do not search for the ones you knew
you do not know the woman standing at the next panel
one white dahlia in her hand

chieu hoi

you betray your mother and father
abandon your wife and child
throw down your rifle
thrown down your name
and come through the perimeter at dusk
now you fight the Cong
you know their names and their families
their field strength and where they hide
you know when they're hungry,
but they are never hungry like you
for when they eat, they become full
but when you eat, you remain empty inside

We were playing a rather unusual, two-base variable ruling sort of softball, witnessed by either the curious or bored Vietnamese locals, when Young unloaded from the executive officer's jeep. He had just returned from Sydney, Australia.

"Hey Leon! How was it?" We yelled. The game, which was not a pressing issue, fell apart and we followed Young down into his hootch, to hear, with the usual ceremony, of his exploits while on R&R. Rest and Relaxation was the official term for one week spent out of country, but most servicemen, as is their fashion, had given it the more accurate abbreviation of I&I, which stood for Intercourse and Intoxication.

Young, with his dark brown, wavy hair and a thick mustache set beneath strong cheek bones which, in themselves, helped set off his deep brown, gold-flecked eyes, stood a stalky five feet ten inches. Like everyone in Vietnam who spent most of a year outside, his skin was yellow brown, with blotches here and there. Everyone who was white, that is. His Gook sores had healed shut and he looked relaxed, if not rested. We sat back, passing a bowl of marijuana among us, to listen to what Young did in Sydney.

"Well, you know, it's really weird being in a civilized place. I mean Sydney, of course. It seemed like an island in the wilderness. I mean, here I am in the bush for seven months, then in twenty-four hours I'm around all these unarmed people wearing clean clothes with all sorts of crazy colors and designs, and shoes too, rather than boots. I saw this guy in a sports jacket and I asked myself, 'Who's he tryin' to kid?' And I almost freaked out when I walked into the can at the airport. It was so clean! I couldn't believe all the porcelain and stainless steel and glass. And there was even this guy in there cleaning it all up even more. I almost felt like hanging around in there for week 'cause it was so clean and squared away."

Someone teased Young about bathrooms. He took a drag off the pipe and went on.

"So anyway, after listening to all the warnings and bullshit at the R&R center they let us go. They told us to watch our money. Everyone would try to take it. Who cares? I checked in at a big hotel at King's Cross where I found more stainless steel and porcelain and a big soft bed and three or four big soft chairs. I got bored real fast so I just went for a long walk.

"I walked all day, all over, and it took me forever to get used to them driving on the left side of the road. You see, usually if you're walking you look to the left for traffic and then cross over or something like that. It's habit, you know, and I swear I almost got wiped out about three times before I got the hang of it. It's odd. I didn't dare drive.

"I took an excursion trip on this boat that went all over the harbor. It's a nice ride, real mellow and you see a lot. It's cheap, too. Anyway, I met this chick on the boat . . ."

Here the guys chimed in with "Dig it, man!" or "There it is!" for that's what most guys wanted to hear. But one guy, who was new in country, drifted away, disenchanted.

". . . and right off she knows I'm a service guy. I guess it was perfectly obvious, but I asked her how she knew anyway."

"'Oh it's easy, Yank,' she told me. 'You seem a bit lost, don't seem to be all quite here.'

"What it all boils down to," Young went on, is that this girl, Jan is her name, invites me to move out of the motel and in with her and her friends who live out by Bondi Beach. It's a good price she wants for a room and some board, so I say, 'Hell yeah!' and we're off to check me out of the hotel.

"Jan had a friend, Mike, who has this really souped-up Falcon with a steering wheel on the right side, really confusing, and he takes us out to this really nice cottage type home, white stucco, red tile roof, green grass, picket fence, the whole thing, and it's got about three girl, some guys and a couple of service dudes staying there. It's a hippie pad. They're playin' rock-and-roll and there's incense burnin' and posters on the walls. Everything. I thought I'd died and gone to heaven or something. I went to this movie with some people from this pad."

Everyone groaned. Someone walked away.

"Hey, listen, man, this wasn't any ordinary flick. This was a Fellini flick. Satyricon was its name but wait 'till you hear the circumstances. Like I was sayin', I was at this hippie pad and about ten minutes after I'm there some girl hands me this little chip about the size of a pin head and tells me it's acid."

Everyone gasped.

"'It's windowpane acid,' she says. So I ate it. Things didn't happen for a while and then we decided to go to this Satyricon because it's supposed to be bizarre, and these folks are into cheap thrills. Before I know it we're in the Falcon and I lose track of where we are. All I know is that we end up at this Italian theater in this Italian neighborhood."

We looked at Young obliquely.

"Really!" Young responded in defense. "Most of the people in the lobby are Italian, or at least they look and speak Italian. By now I'm really off and I'm wonderin' what the fuck is going on. I'm standing against the wall waiting for everyone to go in and Jan comes over and holds my hand.

"'You okay, luv?' She knows I'm tripping and sort of wants to make sure that I don't freak out or anything.

"I say, 'Sure,' and she gives me a little kiss and this little sort of wink and for a second or two things make a little more sense.

"So now things are under control and the movie starts and we all are in a row down close to the front. The whole theater's gabbing away in Italian and Jan's still holding my hand. It's all I can do to stop myself from laughing out insanely. But then I flash back to the day Sugar Bear was killed and I remember the mortar rounds that got those Koreans killed a couple 'a weeks ago. I tell you, the mind's a wild thing, a real untamed monster. I felt like I could see myself sitting there in that theater. I started analyzing everything, faster and faster, everything falling into categories. For a moment everything was fallin' into the hostile category and for some reason Jan seemed to sense it and then she'd give my hand a little squeeze. Finally the feature begins and I realize the goddamn thing's in Italian. It's got English subtitles, but no one needs to bother with them 'cause they're all Italians, anyway, except for a few of us down in front.

"Well, Fellini's bizarre, all right. I couldn't figure out at first what was goin' on and I couldn't read too fast either. First the letters would wiggle around and then if I got them to stop movin' I'd forget how to relate them to the rest of the words and finally if I got a handle on all that, then they'd be off the screen and the scene would change. It was a real violent and chaotic movie I could tell, 'cause of the way the scenes would change and the facial expression. I kept flashin' back to here. I guess I was trying to relate to the reality of the 'Nam because this was all I knew for too long. Can you imagine being in a place for only seven months and havin' it get into you so far that even when you leave, it's all there is?"

We all nodded slowly to respond to Young's question.

He went on. "Then I remembered I was on acid, and it sort of calmed me down. I figured if I didn't know what was goin' on that at least part of it was due to the acid.

"That helped. But I still kept thinking about here and it all seemed like it was just my imagination. How could this be real, the 'Nam, I mean, when here I was sitting in an Italian movie theater in Sydney? These people don't wear uniforms, or boots. They don't carry M-16s or grenade launchers. They don't seem to be concerned about a mortar attack. I mean, what if a sapper came in here and started throwing around satchel charges or something? Shit, they don't even have concertina wire around the ticket booth, and no grenade mesh, either. If this is real, then how can Vietnam be real, too? One reality obliterated the other. War eats peace. Peace is sleep, the sleep of the dead."

"There it is," someone said.

"Man, I hated thinking that way. Know what I mean?"

A few guys nodded.

"'cause it's psychotic to think that way but being in 'Nam's like livin' underwater and peace is the air. You know it's there, but if you try to breath it, you drown.

"Anyway, this movie seemed like somethin' from Mars. Then I saw what was happenin' 'cause I read it before, in a book.

"You see, this woman who was married was tearing her hair out and it was ancient times, like Rome. She's upset 'cause her husband's dead and she's gonna be faithful to his memory forever. Her friends try to tell her it's cool to enjoy life even though her husband died but she's really got herself convinced that she's doin' the right thing.

"So, the point of the story is, you see, that this young Roman stud of soldier, who's been assigned to guard her husband's tomb, I guess he was a fat cat or somethin', fucks here right there on top of the casket, or whatever they used in those days, and all of a sudden she realizes that she's gotta whole lot of livin' to do and she runs off with this stud. I suppose they lived happily ever after, too, but Fellini didn't say anything about that.

"When I saw that part of the film, I just shook my head and laughed at how stupid we all must be if a story this old still needs to be told in a theater, sittin' in the twentieth century. But then here I am, I thought, sittin' in a war that's probably as old as when the story took place and so what if there's airplanes and rockets and fucking television when it's still a matter of kill or be killed, love or hate. I started thinking about my old girlfriend who sort of dumped me before I came to 'Nam.

"You know? It don't mean jack shit to me now, but I was all busted up when she gave me the shaft. I didn't even have enough gumption to stay out of the Army and . . ."

Here one guy interrupted Young, trying to point out that it took gumption to do your duty and that anyone who avoided the draft was gutless. We told him to shut up because he was acting stupid. He left. We had, for the most part, come to the common understanding that none of us, at least, knew what duty was.

". . . and so I got drafted. I sort of blamed it on Rose, that was her name, but now I realize that I put myself here. I think I know why, too, sort of. What's ironic about Rose, though, is that she got interested in this older guy who really had the bucks. I had some bucks, 'cause I worked, but not like this guy."

"What's ironic about a chick goin' for the bucks?" someone asked.

"It's ironic because this guy had just made his bucks by inventing some sort of synthetic blood, or something. He was sellin' it to the government, to pump up the biggest blood market of the day, the 'Nam. So I get all shit-faced and sent to 'Nam because Rose falls for this guy's bucks who's gettin' rich fillin' up us poor assholes. It's great. Somebody should write a story about it."

Young went outside for a minute. A guy lit up another bowl and passed it around.

Young continued when he came back. "Finally Satyricon is over and we go to this disco bar where all there is is GIs and their whores. I'm bummed out. All this is the same old shit as far as I'm concerned. Besides, I begin to realize I dig the bush, man. I'm somebody out here 'cause I'm myself. In Sydney, all I am is what my billfold says I am. But this Jan's been sticking with me and she asks me if I want to split or eat somethin' and I said, yeah.

"We walk to a fancy Italian restaurant and Jan sees right away that I'm not too impressed. But I like Italian food anyway and I ask her to stay with me and eat. I liked her. She was a round eye, and she was someone different to talk to. She wasn't too shy about asking me about 'Nam. She'd been with lots of guys fresh out of 'Nam and she had some pretty hairy stories about what they did and said. One guy busted her up pretty bad once, but she didn't seem too uptight about it. Anyway, I tried to tell her what it's like here, but shit, I'm no writer or actor. I couldn't really say much. I mean, I didn't really feel like reporting body counts to her or telling her how much the Vietnamese hate us, so what else is there?

"I started rapping about drugs. She said she found it hard to believe how guys could come down and eat acid for a week and then go back to 'Nam. Guys told her about how good the pot is here. I told her that we called it 'dew.' She didn't know that. Anyway, how cheap it is and that there's so much of it. And the smack, she knew heroin was smack, and Number Tens and opium and speed. She guessed that the Chinese were conducting chemical warfare against us and, you know, I think she's got a point there.

"But I got to asking her questions about Australia and about her. She wasn't from Sydney. She was from Murra Murra, which is in Queensland, sort of isolated. She was in Sydney to go to school and, well, she decided to get herself another sort of education and became, as she put it, a girl of the streets. She said she missed home, hadn't been there in over a year. She kept rapping about it so I told her I'd go there with her, give her some money and stuff, if she sort of stayed with me and not ditch me in the middle of fucking Queensland. She thought a minute and then agreed.

"That was a great decision 'cause I had a hell of a time on the way there and back. We didn't spend too much time there 'cause it's a long way there. We borrowed a van or actually we talked some people into goin' up there with us who had a van so we packed a bunch of stuff and forgot about Sydney. One of the guys who went with us was a botany student from Sweden. He claimed there were psilocybin mushrooms up in a certain part of Queensland. Actually, it was real close to Jan's home, so we went there with a double purpose. What a trip. We were all eating acid and had this sorry-ass dew they were smoking. I couldn't believe it. They paid five bucks for a matchbox full and it was nuthin' but camel shit. But then we were so fucking blitzed on acid that I'm sure it wouldn't have made any difference. I kept flashin' on 'Nam. You know, little bits and pieces, scenes and faces. I couldn't believe I wasn't here, in 'Nam, and I couldn't believe I was where I was. Lost in space. If they would have let me off, there in the outback, I guess it was the outback, I would have felt like I was on Mars. It was all alien, everything, especially me. Man, what a terrain they have there, talk about thick! There was this kind of underbrush that stood about ten feet high, and it was all twisted around everything. It was nuthin' but underbrush and road and every once in a while some straight up and down cliff would come up on the horizon and the road would have to go off at a right angle just to get around it. Then there would be these little settlements along the road every twenty miles or so. We stopped at about everyone just to see what it was like 'cause it was all new to most of us.

"It took us a full day to get up around Murra Murra. Along with stopping at towns we kept stopping along the way looking for mushrooms whenever this crazy Swedish botanist thought that the conditions looked right. I didn't really care. My head was clearing up and the air was fresh and clean. It's cool down there this time of year. Things are backward down there. They even said whirlpools swirled in the opposite direction south of the equator, but I never noticed. It's not backward, I guess, only different.

"Anyway, this one chick kept callin' the GIs "Yank" more than she really had to and this one dude got upset. He asked her if she had any idea of where Georgia was, and she said she thought it was somewhere in the Ukraine. It was a laugh a minute, but after every laugh I'd sort of give myself a reality check. I kept relating everything to the 'Nam. It's hard not to categorize things into hostile or friendly when you've been at it for a while. I'll tell you dudes something right now, if you don't already know it. If you don't think the 'Nam gets into you, all the way through to your backbone and out around for more, just leave this place. You'll find out. It's in your soul, man. I know I'm gonna think about this place for fucking ever.

"Well, we never did get any mushrooms to eat. Lars, that's what we called this drug-crazed botanist, found a few mushrooms that looked just about right but none of us dared eat 'em. He said they just as easily have been poisonous as hell. It's nice to know that your common sense works even when you're high on acid in the middle of the outback and switching from one reality to another and you're weighing them in a balance scale. We didn't need to eat any mushrooms anyway. I was getting tired of tripping about then and besides, your body can only handle it for so long. Then it doesn't matter how much you do 'cause you just can't get off anymore."

It began to get dark at the firebase. Some of us had to gear up for guard. That night we expected activity. The two infantry squads that had been staying outside our perimeter were setting out listening posts and ambushes in another sector. We were down to two howitzers, with support from the Quad .50s. No one bothered thinking about being overrun. It was a matter of infiltration and sapper attacks. Listening to Young ramble on was good. Our eyes filled with the Vietnam stare, and we thought ten years ahead of ourselves. Young's voice drew us back, in close proximity to the present.

"We spent a few nights in Queensland," Young went on, "and then decided to head back to Bondi Beach. All I wanted to do was lay back for a while or go on a long walk through Sydney. I really dug the outback, but after 'Nam when you see a trail, you think you better stay off it, or when you see a valley, you know you should stay out of it. It's all bullshit if you're not fighten' a war. It's paranoia. I'm afraid to go back to the World, in a way."

We all looked at him.

"You always hear about these 'Nam vets that freak out when they get back. It's the only ones you ever do hear about, it seems. Like that dude in Austin or somewhere in Texas. You get the idea that somebody who never saw a firefight, or somebody get blown up just really doesn't know what's happenin' and that's just sick, man. And then you get these dudes that say, 'Well I saw it all in World War Two and look at me. I'm okay, so why are these Vietnam creeps acting so different?'"

Young shrugged his shoulders. "I don't know. Maybe it's television.

"One of the last days I was there I spent the whole day on the beach. It was sort of cold, but I had a wool sweater and some jeans. Man, did that feel far out wearing something other than OD. I stayed so clean. I just sat there watching the gulls and the shorebirds. Not too many people were on the beach but a few guys in wet suits were body surfing. The surf, if you sit there long enough, has this continual roar that never changes except in the wind a little bit. It's always there.

"That night when I went back to the house I listened for the surf and I could hear it 'cause I knew what to listen for. But it was great on the beach that day. If I got hungry, I'd just walk over to a café or a stand or something. No fucking line.

"I bought a small book and read the whole thing that day. Just sitting and reading or watching the surf, with the surf roaring all the time. I only thought of the 'Nam about every fifteen seconds.

"Once, when I was sitting on the beach, this guy comes up to me and very friendly like he starts talkin' about the weather and body surfing. I asked him to sit down. He was from Darwin and was in Sydney on business. I wondered to myself what business would bring him to Bondi Beach, for I knew it was a hangout for homosexuals. Maybe he thought I was one. I don't know. When I told him I was from the States he wanted to know about back in the World. Right away he falls into a political philosophical conversation. I didn't mind, but I really couldn't say much. I mean, there I was, watching the gulls when all of a sudden, this stranger comes up to me and before I know it he starts layin' all this political stuff on me. I hate politics anyway. I figure that no situation ever has to be political. It only gets political 'cause people want to complicate things with economics and religion. I can't ever think of the right thing to say when someone starts rappin' to me about politics. I can usually think of something later and then I say, 'Yeah, I should go find that guy, or whatever, and tell 'em what I really think. But timing, as it is in love, is everything.

"This guy had the idea that the U.S. was on its way down. I'm so used to badmouthing the U.S. that out of habit I agreed with him. But way down inside it kind of stirred something up. It wasn't really politics or patriotism either. It was like crying over the good earth where I was raised. I want to see my land living and breathing under a real, fresh layer of peace, you know? It's not borders I'm talkin' about. It's just the landscape that I know from birth stretching out to the world and then sending the signal of peace to the universe. Maybe then the good spirits would come back. It seems like the bad spirits are in control now."

Someone said amen.

"Fuck that shit, man. It's not a matter of religion., except where spirituality is involved. I mean, can you really respect a clergyman who's layin' some sermon on you about how good God is when right behind him we got a fire mission goin' on that's blowin' the fuck out of other human beings? It gets old real fast. I'm talkin' about the bad spirits that come from inside us and that we're responsible for. They're in control, or we're lettin' them be in control. Peace is where it's at."

Young reached for the bowl and took a deep drag.

"This guy from Darwin thought that we were a lot weaker, militarily, I guess, than we appear. Otherwise, why were we still fuckin' around in Southeast Asia? Why don't we just mop up? He said 'Nam was sort of symbolic of our weakness and I think he was pleased about it. Or maybe he was pleased 'cause he thought it made him look smart to say that sort of thing. I felt like layin' out the whole scene to him the way I see it. I don't think he could ever comprehend all the money that goes down the tube here in 'Nam.

"If the 'Nam's doing anything, what it's doing is breaking the bank. Not only of money, but of ways to make money. I mean, sure, you can have a hell of a war machine, but the way we're runnin' things, the only return we're gettin' is a bunch of body bags and a bunch of pissed off people. Let's put it this way. If you cut down a tree, then someone can have a house or stay warm or read a book or about a million other things. If you mine some iron ore, you can turn it into a car or a tank. The car could be all right, but there isn't much of a return on a tank. I know that makin' a tank keeps people workin' but that's where all this bad spirituality comes in, you see. You just can't keep pumping up this war machine without the shit hittin' the fan, in a spiritual sense. That's why we can't win this war, 'cause now the shit's hittin' the fan. It's why the 'Nam's in our soul."

Another guy left and the group listening to Young dwindled to his close friends, the ones who had known each other the longest and the ones who would be going home soonest.

"Mr. Chips, that's what I called his guy from Darwin, was really all right. He started me thinkin'. And it's good to hear another point of view. A dude gets confused when one newspaper says one thing and the next one contradicts it and what you see in front of you tells you both papers are full of shit. What do you do when some idiot politician rambles on for a couple of years and then you find out he's lying? And the hippies aren't any better. They think the Cong are saints or something, or that every GI's got innocent guts hanging' from his teeth.

"I did a lot of watchin' and listenin' before I got drafted. Man, I couldn't make any decisions, except that I knew, or felt that sure, it's wrong to be in Vietnam, but what can I do? If I had the chance, maybe I'd have gone to Canada. In some ways I think it takes more guts to do that than to just go ahead and take your chances in the service."

"Dig it, man. There it is," we replied in support.

"But I didn't know anyone who could help me get there. Besides, I didn't have the bucks. I was working but I didn't have any money saved."

Young was soul searching and we knew it was something that we all must do, at times, when your soul is doing battle with what Young had named bad spirits. We let him go, as we knew Young would have let any of us go. We were friends, and this is what friends were for.

"I guess all through basic and artillery training, even though the lifers kept saying we were going' to 'Nam, I kept sayin', 'Nah, this won't happen to me.' But then when we were in formation and they read out my orders for 'Nam, what a 'stroke to the groin area,' as the saying goes. But you know? I'm sort of glad I got sent here rather than to Europe and stateside or whatever."

We all remembered the grenade that someone rolled into the chief of smoke's hootch with a note on it, 'Next time we pull the pin, shit head!' Three days later we had a new chief.

"I don't know what it is about this place. It seems like the Vietnamese are fighting a different war than we are. We got tons of fire power and the sky belongs to us. My drill sergeant was right though. The night belongs to Charlie, and everything underground, too. It's their home, man. Can you dig it? Half the time I don't even know what direction I'm facing. That never happened at home. I had natural instinct. Over here I got a perpetual case of vertigo even when I'm on the ground. I get this weird idea that our great fucking war machine, the Green Machine, was getting a little rusty so the generals poured poison in the idiot politicians' ears, you know. 'You better watch out, man,' they whispered to the big ducks in the east, 'like, if we don't kick ass in Southeast Asia, pretty soon it's gonna be all Communist and then . . .' Then what? That's what I'd like to know. So fucking what? Nuthin' but a broken record, man, a broken record. God, people must be paranoid of the United States. We're so unpredictable. Who else would drop a nuclear device on two big cities? And in the name of fucking peace! What a burn."

Young was getting agitated, and we could see the Vietnam stare lying dead still in his eyes. He was beginning to realize he was back in Vietnam. He was gone and now he was back. Nothing less than an injury or time could release him. Except, of course, death. It never did too much good for anyone to talk as Young was talking, or to talk it all. But you couldn't stop them, and in many cases, the ones who never talked at all about how they felt ended up doing crazy, dangerous and evil things. We tried to relax Young. The marijuana helped, maybe. But we knew that marijuana was used as a coping mechanism, used for exactly the same reason as alcohol and heroin.

"Mr. Chips seemed to represent the opinion of the rest of the world." Young went on. "Like the rest of the world's just waiting for us to stumble and fall and then it's the vultures to the meat time. My how time flies. One kingdom reaches the top of the heap. It does its thing, topples and it's replaced by another one. Who'll be the next in line? What are we compared to ten thousand years of history?"

Young shook his head. We told him everything was all right, that we felt like shit, too. He laughed. His eyes lit up, burning off the stare.

"Hey you guys. The last night I was in Sydney I did a lot of thinkin' about what to bring back here for you. I talked to Jan about it. I don't know, she just seemed like the type you can talk to. She's off the wall, but she's all right. She moves slow at night in a dark room if she thinks you're sleeping. But you're not, 'cause you know someone's there. I didn't ask here what to bring back, only if what I was thinkin' of bringing back was done very much."

We asked him what he brought back. Young reached in his pants pocket and brought out a small medicine bottle. He held it up to the fading sunlight that streamed through the door. In it were six small translucent chips.

"Windowpane," Young said. "Jan thinks maybe a dozen or so guys have brought it back in the last year. What do you think?"

toy soldiers

what came before,
and what came after
they're all linked by the 'Nam
as a child you play with toy soldiers
move them around
pronounce them dead, and then bring them back
until they begin to move on their own
begin to take shape, and then to take aim
until you become a soldier
and someone pronounces you dead

ARVN

some are like you
just trying to remain in one piece
but they are never in one piece
two ARVN boys in the market place
brother or cousins,
or maybe just friends
they stand close together
holding hands, not talking, not smiling
and then you understand
they're saying goodbye
maybe for the last time

Central Highlands

the sirens of Titan scream
and the fire mission begins
you repeat the ARVN's coordinates
and wonder if he has them right
but he's called the mission down on himself
and it's over after just one round
you kneel in remorse
while your piety goes unnoticed

Montagnards

you call them the Degar
you name them the White Elephant Division
you give them small arms, and mountain howitzers
train them how to fight in the night
but for the Degar,
there is no South or North Vietnam
they make no distinctions between warring factions
they just kill them all
and let you sort them out

The Desertion of Wiley Blooms

The infantry, which had set out its own listening posts for the night, reported activity. So, at eleven, Lopez, who was now only a buck private, was ordered to man a new guard bunker. He meandered between the gun pits of his artillery unit thinking about his girlfriend and the next evening, which would probably be as starry as this one, when he would visit her in the village below the firebase. He hummed her favorite tune. The powdery red sand puffed out beneath his boots as he walked. The air was calm. The dust spewed up around his legs and was illuminated by stars and a sliver of bright new moon. Sometimes it's so peaceful here, he thought, still humming. But then he stopped and crouched down by a retaining wall. That's an M-16, he knew, fired from within the firebase. He did not see any muzzle flashes or hear any bullets snap past him, so he guessed it was a troop who was drunk or drugged, maybe both. Not much to worry about, hearing rifles fired into the night. It was a way to vent despair, or to state a certain lack of faith. Maybe it was the intangible effect of the elements of combat which, at times, were dominant in one's behavior and at other times subtle. It could get out of control, usually while drinking. There was also heroin and the barbiturates which could be bought in the village below. Realizing it was all in a night's work, Lopez began humming again and strolled out to the guard bunker.

When he reached his post, he made sure to make a little sound or two to warn anyone who might be in the bunker. No one responded. He felt for the steps with a probing toe of his boot. He found what he wanted and slung his rifle over his shoulder with the machine gun balanced on his shoulder. He twisted his lanky body sideways to negotiate the steep, narrow and invisible steps that led down into the side of the mountain. More shots from above, on the level of the firebase, filtered into the bunker. They seemed distant, and even more irrelevant than before. He placed the M-60 in its tripod and unslung the bandolier from around his chest. This only happens in the movies, he thought, and grunted a short, unhappy laugh, as he locked and loaded in the dark. His hands felt for and found the detonators. They were for land mines that were also dug into the side of the mountain. By now his eyes had adjusted to the dim light. Everything was in place, for waiting and testing.

The shooting had stopped by now, and the firebase above him was still. He pulled a small olive drab canvas bag full of marijuana from a cargo pocket and brought out a Zippo lighter. As he lit his pipe a can bounced on the roof of the bunker. "Who?" he yelled. "Nugent" from above. Lopez kept his pipe going, and it dissipated its ember glow along the walls of the bunker. As Nugent entered, Lopez offered him the pipe.

"Thanks."

"What's all that shooting about?"

"Wiley Blooms."

Lopez stopped smoking. "Oh great. Did he quit on his own? I doubt it."

"No. Somebody coldcocked him. I guess they're gonna trash him."

A voice from above called for Lopez.

"Yeah? What d'ya want?"

"Wanna talk t'ya, 'at's all."

"Blooms? What's goin' on? What you doin' here?"

Blooms stumbled down the steps and into the bunker. Lopez and Nugent watched him as he felt for where he stood. Lopes prepared another pipe and offered it to Blooms, but he did not notice it.

"Nugent here says you stepped on your dick again. You under arrest or something?"

Blooms belched. "Yeah. But they left me alone for a minute, thought I was passed out."

"What are you doin' here then?" Nugent asked.

"Gonna get in more trouble for that, and get us in trouble, too," I added.

Blooms wrapped his big hand around Nugent's shoulder. "Now jes' be quiet, Nugent. I ain't gonna take long, an' I wanna' talk to Lopez here for a minute." He was polite and waited for a reply.

Nugent shifted his eyes to see his shoulder, so valueless in Blooms's gentle but coercive grasp. "Sure Blooms, I just don't want any trouble, that's all I mean. I'll be goin' home in a month, and it seems wherever you hang out there's . . ."

Blooms patted Nugent on the back. "Forget it man, I jes' . . ."

Lopez took another draw on his pipe, and it lit up Blooms's face. The left side was swollen, and his eye was almost shut.

"Hey!" Lopez interrupted. "You really got pasted, Wiley. Sorry."

Blooms let go of Nugent. "What the hell you sorry for? You didn't do it, and you ain't feelin' it either."

Lopez stood up. "All right. All right. Just don't get jumpy, Wiley." He put his hand on the bolt of the machine gun. "It's too crowded down here to go grabbin' people." He took one more draw on the pipe and passed it to Nugent. "Now, Wiley, what do you want down here anyway?"

"You know I had guard again tonight?" Blooms asked.

Lopez shrugged his shoulders.

"That makes forty-three nights in a row." He stood up straight and looked Lopez in the eyes, as if to ask, what do you think about that?'

"So you got drunk instead, so they couldn't make you pull guard again?"

Blooms nodded. Nugent giggled and passed the pipe back to Lopez. Lopez offered it to Blooms, who refused.

"Well, you know, Wiley, we've talked about this before."
He sighed. "I still don't know much about the situation."

"What situation is that?" Nugent asked.

"Well," Lopez went on, "Blooms here seems to think
he's bein' discriminated against. You know, bein' an
Indian and everything." He turned to Nugent. "What do
you think? Think Blooms here's been on guard so long
'cause he's an Indian?"

Blooms grunted.

Nugent cleared his throat. "Sure. I mean, why the hell
not? Blooms gets a lot of guard duty all right, and Lopez,
you sure as hell get a lot of shit duty for bein' a pot head,
and me, hah! I was supposed to be a god damn chaplain's
assistant, and then they go and change my orders; got my
ass sent here. And I got thirty days left here, and what
happens? My wife, she writes me this god damn letter . .
."

"What the hell you gettin' at, Nugent. Lopez asked you
'bout 'scrimination and . . ."

"What he's gettin' at is this Wiley, you got a problem?
Tough shit."

Blooms spun around and went for Lopez. But Lopez
ducked and moved in behind him, slipped his arms under
Blooms's armpits and then grabbed behind the neck in a
full nelson.

"Blooms! Blooms! I was jus' kiddin' man. I'm sorry,
mellow out for Christ's sake!"

Nugent tried to grab Blooms's arms, but Blooms threw
him off and started banging head on the mantel of the
retaining wall, lifting Lopez off the ground as he swung
down.

Lopez yelled at Nugent. "Get those detonators off the
sandbags before he sets the whole god . . ."

The top of the firebase lit up, and the explosion
deafened the three men in the bunker as mud and shale

blew back. They covered their ears and rolled around on the dirt floor.

"Jesus Christ!"

"Wow!"

"What happened?"

"Go to hell, Blooms."

Echoes returned from the surrounding mountains, and they heard generators starting and lights coming on, or turning off, on the firebase and the village below.

"Get on the horn, Nugent, and tell 'em we're okay. Tell 'em it was all a big mistake."

"Do it yourself, Lopez. Blooms came to see you, man. He's your friend, not mine."

"Listen man! I taking Blooms to his hootch 'cause if the battery commander finds out he's here, he's . . ."

"What the hell should I'm tell 'em when you ain't here?"

"I'm takin'a leak, or somethin'. Anything, I don' care."

He helped Blooms up and out of the bunker. Blooms groped along and was having trouble finding his way.

"You okay, Wiley?"

"What happened back there, anyway? We get hit or somethin'?"

"It's more like, or somethin'."

"What do you mean?"

Lopez stopped and Blooms piled into him. "Wiley, you know damn well what happened. You detonated that Claymore mine."

"Oh, 'at's what I thought."

Lopez started walking again, in between the gun pits and the ammunition bunkers. Blooms stood still, watching him as he strolled along. He stopped again and turned to Blooms.

"Come on, Wiley, let's go to your hootch so you don't get in anymore trouble. Come on."

"You said 'tough shit' to me, Oscar. You don't give a damn that I been on guard forty-three nights in a row. You don't . . ."

"Hey, man, let's talk about it later, okay? You got to lay low tonight. You can't be runnin' around blowing off Claymores and screamin' at me in the middle of the firebase. People are gonna get the wrong impression. So come on!"

Blooms thought for a moment, then caught up to Lopez. They walked back to Blooms's hootch. He was falling asleep by the time Lopez helped him onto his cot. He rolled over on his back and hung his hand down on the dirt floor and a cock roach scurried over to investigate. Lopez ground it into the dirt with his boot, then rested Blooms's hand back on his chest. He held it there for a short moment, then left for his guard bunker.

A can banged. "Who?"

"Lopez."

Nugent offered him the pipe as he sat down in the bunker.

"Well?" asked Nugent.

"He's out. I hope for the night. Who came around?"

"The damn battery commander, that's who."

"What'd he say?"

"Wants you to report to the first sergeant."

"Top? When?"

"Now, I guess."

"Christ."

Lopez leaned back on the bench. He lit another pipe and looked out over the desultory lights of Dalat which, after nothing came of the explosions, drifted off to sleep again. Rain clouds began forming above the hamlet that sat at the base of the mountain. The clouds crept up the face of the mountain, snuffing out, one by one, the remaining lights. Soon the clouds would find Lopez. And the clouds would condense on his face and weapons and perhaps, he thought, the rain clouds will snuff out my remaining lights. He sighed and took another puff on his pipe.

Not much time passed, Lopez thought maybe five minutes, and then Nugent broke the silence.

"Don't you think you better go? The BC said he'd come looking for you if you didn't show up at the first sergeant's hootch."

"So?"

"So don't be a fool, Lopez. You know the BC's out to hang your ass if he can. And the first sergeant's always sending you out on those damn patrols. He thinks you're Hispanic or something."

"Spooky patrols, no sense to them at all. Maybe I am Hispanic."

"There it is, man. So why don't you avoid the hassle of them coming down here to get you? Besides, I don't want any more action down here tonight."

"Yeah, you're right. I'm gonna go, but I've been thinkin' about Blooms."

Maybe I'm his only friend, Lopez thought. Maybe he came out here 'cause I was his only friend. "He's pretty damn sensitive."

"Yeah? So's my asshole."

Lopez laughed.

"You better get going."

He climbed out of the bunker and looked around the firebase. On top it was clear as he strolled along, he watched the moon leading a star through a pass in the mountains. His path took him to the edge of the firebase, overlooking the far side from the hamlet. The rocks and sand on the near slope of Hill 507 glowed in the pale luminescence or were hidden darkly is shadows behind the shrub conifers of the central highlands. An old, French-styled chalet, battered by American and North Vietnamese artillery, floated into view. He wondered where the people were who once lived there. Probably in Dalat, he thought. But will they ever be happy again? Hell, they're obviously rich, so who the hell cares? And he felt guilty about feeling that way about the people who used to live in the chalet. I wonder what's worse, he continued, worrying about yourself too much, or worrying about others too much?

The first sergeant's hootch came up on the left. Light shot through the cracks in the door and he could hear the battery commander and the first sergeant talking inside. Then from behind her heard the chief of the firing battery.

"Lopez, is that you?"

"Right, Smoke. What's goin' on?"

"Was Blooms down in the bunker when the Claymore went off?"

"Who told you that, Smoke?"

"Come on in. We been waitin' for you."

The chief of the firing battery held the door open for Lopez, who shrugged his shoulders, sighed out loud, and went in.

The first sergeant stopped talking. All three of them stared at Lopez, who began humming his girlfriend's favorite tune. They frowned, and he stopped. But still they said nothing, so he decided to get them to speak.

"Do you believe in karma?"

"Why did you leave your post, Lopez?" the first sergeant asked.

"Had to take a leak."

"Did Blooms detonate that Claymore?"

"Who told you that?"

"Never mind who told me that, God damn it!" The first sergeant turned to the battery commander and shook his head.

The battery commander kept staring at Lopez. "We know Blooms was in that bunker. Did you know he's under guard?"

"I haven't seen him tonight. Why you talkin' to me 'bout all this? Who's supposed to be guardin' him?"

"Never mind that either!" the first sergeant yelled.

"Hey mellow out man. I mean ah . . ."

"Just be quiet Lopez," the battery commander said, "and listen up." He cleared his throat. "Lopez, we've decided that you should guard Blooms."

The conversation died. Lopez blinked and stared at the three men in the hootch. They returned his stare, and each smirked a bit as they observed Lopez's reactions. The fire direction control generator started, giving them all a reason to finish the conversation.

"Me? Guard Blooms?"

They nodded.

"I'm only an E-2. I can't guard anybody."

"But this is an emergency Lopez. I don't have any NCOs to spare. I need them on the guns. I'm giving you a direct order, Lopez. Guard Blooms." The battery commander spun around and left the hootch.

Lopez scowled, shook his head, and rubbed his nose while facing the two sergeants. "This is illegal, you know. Isn't it?"

"No, Lopez, not illegal, just irregular, that's all. But like the captain said, we can't afford to send any NCOs along to escort that damn fool Indian Blooms to the stockade. What's the matter? Don't you want to get out of the war for a while, Lopez?"

Lopez remained silent, shuffling a boot along in the dirt, waiting for more of an explanation that he knew would never come from the first sergeant.

"Now listen up," the first sergeant continued, "you stay on Blooms tonight. He's your responsibility. Don't let him get in any more trouble. In the morning, at 05:30, you're taking him out of here, to Long Binh Jail. I'll have travel orders for you in the morning. I want you at the landing zone at 05:15 and I'll have your special orders. Chief here will fill you in. Now get out . . ."

"But how the hell am I supposed to get him all the way to . . ."

"Come on, Lopez," the chief of smoke interrupted, "I'll explain all this outside."

Lopez glared at the first sergeant, who had turned his back. Then he walked out into the night, where the chief of smoke was waiting for him.

"Smoke? What the hell's goin' on here?"

"Take it easy, take it easy. First off, go get your rifle and your gear from your guard bunker, stow it, and meet at my hootch in five minutes. I got somebody else takin' your guard. Now git!"

In five minutes, Lopez was standing in front of chief of smoke's hootch. He coughed so that he could be heard.

"That you, Lopez?"

"Yeah."

"Well come on in. I ain't got all night."

He walked in.

"Now, Lopez? What's botherin' you 'bout takin' Blooms to jail?"

"Bothern' me? I don't want to take anyone to jail. I don't wanna take Wiley to LBJ. It's insane. It's a job for a lifer, or at least some sort of sergeant. I mean, why me? Why choose me to take him away?"

Chief of smoke sat back in his easy chair, a makeshift collection of mosquito netting, hammock mesh and duffle bag, and lit a cigarette. "Why you, Lopez? That's easy. 'cause both you and Blooms is a pain in the BC's ass."

Lopez was about to speak up, but the chief of smoke cut him short. "Now I know you do your job. You ain't bad on the guns. And Blooms, he does his share over in ammo section. But the BC, he's got a case a' the ass 'bout both of ya. So's the first sergeant. I don't what you done, but they both just as soon see you both gone, 'least for a while, anyway. The BC, he don't like pot heads like you, and Blooms can't be trusted anymore. BC don't work with the firing battery like I do, so he really don't know what's goin' on in the pits. Besides, he don't want you gunnin' anymore. He just about shit when he found out an E-2 was gunnin' in section three, meanin' you. He wants an NCO in that job. It would be his ass, and mine too, if gun three fired out and blew away some friendlies. An E-2 can't be held responsible for firing out. Me? I think you're a good enough gunner. It don't make no difference what rank a gunner is, long as he knows what he's doin'. I guess they figure Blooms will be gone for at least a month on pre-trial confinement. And you, maybe they hope you get lost, or somethin'."

"Get lost or somethin'?" Lopez scratched his cheek and narrowed his eyes. "That sounds like a good idea. Do you think . . ."

"But that ain't all, Lopez. You got the detail for another reason too." The chief of smoke was smiling at Lopez.

"Oh?"

"You see, I tol' 'em you was the man for the job."

Lopez dropped his shoulders and sighed.

"'cause he and you is friends. He listens to you, maybe."

"Ha! Blooms doesn't listen to a soul. He's alone."

"I know he's alone. He ain't got none of his kind in the battery. A black man, he got some blacks around. Maybe they's friends, maybe they hate each other. Who knows? But Blooms ain't got no Indians 'round to like or hate."

"So why me, Smoke? I'm not Indian either . . ."

"I know that. But 'least he hears you. You closer 'n anyone else in the battery. And like I said, the BC and the first sergeant like to get you both out 'a their hair."

Lopez shook his head. "You know, when Blooms finds out he's goin' in for pre-trial confinement and that I'm the one escorting him to LBJ, he'll walk right away from me, and I won't stop him. I wouldn't know how." He turned to leave.

"Wait now, Lopez, I got what you need." The chief of smoke walked over to his footlocker, unlocked it, and brought out an ammunition can. He smiled again at Lopez, then dumped a holstered forty-five semi-automatic pistol, and three loaded clips onto his cot. "Know how to use this?"

"Sure, I guess. You want me to use that on Blooms?"

"Probably won't have to if he knows you have it."

"Are you sure about all of this Smoke? I mean, what if Wiley just decides to split, never come back?"

"Ain't any of my business, Lopez. But like I said, the BC, he just as soon be rid a' ya for good. Same with the first sergeant. Now you remember to pick up orders in the mornin', right?"

"Right."

"Okay. Now you go hook up with Blooms, and don't you let him out a' your sight. Stick to 'em like glue, you hear?"

Lopez nodded and was about to leave.

"Now don't go forgettin' this pistol, Lopez, damn it!"

He turned around. "Oh, right."

"I don't know what you're thinkin', Lopez, but you best get it out a' your head, whatever it is. You just keep your mind on the job, and don't get no fancy ideas."

The field phone squawked.

"Smoke? FDC. We have contact in sector five and they want high explosives and illumination in five minutes. Get 'em ready."

The chief of smoke acknowledged the call, then turned to Lopez, "You do what I say, Lopez, everything's gonna be okay. Now go."

Lopez watched him as he ran out of his hootch with a flashlight and a transit. He heard him yelling at men as they ran by. Then he sat down on the cot and examined the pistol, turning it this way and that in his hand, aiming it, and sliding the action. He replaced it. In the gun pits men were yelling, and dogs, running along the top of the sandbags, were barking. There was considerable swearing and Lopez sighed and looked at the pistol again. He scratched his cheek and narrowed his eyes again, then put his hand down on the clips that lay on the cot. He collected them and stuffed then in his cargo jacket pocket. Then he dropped the pistol in the cargo pocket of his pants and left the hootch.

The hootch, where the ammunition section slept, was deserted except for Blooms. He was still sleeping, but Lopez knew that when the fire mission began, he would wake up. The guns were aligned over the top of the ammunition section's hootch, and no one could sleep, or remained passed out, through the concussion produced by guns that close. Number two gun was about to register, and Lopez could hear the radio man yelling orders. Finally, "Number Two, Fire!" He could tell they were loading a high charge by the noise and shock of the report. Blooms's cot jumped. The ground quaked beneath the gun and the surrounding area. Blooms fell half out of his cot and tried to roll back next to the sandbags that served as a wall. He mumbled to himself.

Lopez interrupted him. "Wiley? Wake up, man. There's a fire mission goin' on right over the hootch. Sounds like a long one, too."

Blooms sat up, rubbing his good eye and gently pawing his swollen one. "Fire mission? Gotta get to work. Man, I never get any sleep." He leaned over to pull the light switch. The bare, incandescent bulb lit up the olive drab and black cell that served as his quarters. It smelled of spent powder from an M-16. They both looked at the damage done by Blooms's M-16 earlier that night. A small, round shaving mirror had been smashed. Its shards flew all over the room, reflecting the light bulb. The mirror's frame still hung from a nail in the wall. Sandbags, gashed open by churning, tumbling M-16 rounds, were slowly draining their contents onto the floor, a shelf, the cot, a helmet. Several bullet holes let in light from the next room through Blooms's poncho that served as a door.

"Nice work, Wiley. Artistic, sensitive, savage, a real . . ."

"Shut up, Oscar. You piss me off."

Just then number two gun fired again. Sand sprinkled down from the damaged bags and the timbers of the hootch shivered.

"Let's go to my hootch. You can crash over there. So far they're only shootin' sector five and I don't think they'll swing all the way around."

Blooms stood up and took a drink from his canteen. "I thought you was on guard. What you doin' over here?"

"Take a guess."

"I don't know. I know I'm pissed at ya. I thought we was friends, and then you pull that 'tough shit' stuff on me. I never tol' that when you was new in country. I never called you a cherry boy. So now you got yer feet under ya and all of a sudden ol' Wiley's just a bag a' shit. So I don't even care why . . ."

"Oh, knock it off, Wiley, will ya? I didn't know you were so upset when you came by. I'm sorry . . ."

"No, you ain't, man."

"Well . . ."

"Don't do no good bein' sorry."

"All right, okay, but let's get the hell out a' here. They're about to adjust the whole damn battery over this hootch."

"I still gotta load ammo."

Then they heard the chief of smoke yelling, "Battery, Fire!" What was left of the mirror frame fell off the wall. A sandbag in the ceiling gave out completely, disemboweling itself on Blooms's cot. They left the hootch just after the salvo and before there was time for another. By the time they reached Lopez's hootch the battery was firing at each gun's pace, in a syncopated star cluster rhythm, and there were unnatural flashes along the ground. And on a distant hill they saw smaller flashes among the rocks and shrubs, followed by soft, almost peaceful reports. Another unit began firing illumination rounds that seemed almost suspended in air as they floated down hanging from small parachutes and creating huge, garish shadows on the landscape.

"Someone's buyin' it out there tonight, Wiley."

"Yeah. Who d'ya think's callin' it in?"

"Some grunts that moved in this evening. Cambodians, I think."

They climbed down the stairs and walked into Lopez's room.

"I still gotta load ammo, Oscar. Why d'ya want me to come over here?"

Lopez cleared his throat. "I don't know how to tell you this, Wiley."

"Quit messin' with your pipe and tell me. And if ya say somethin' about bein' sorry again . . ."

"You don't even know why I'm gonna say I'm sorry, but you might as well know now, as in the morning."

"Know what?" Blooms was about to leave, but then he sat down.

"Short and sweet, Wiley, you messed up one too many times with your M-16. BC figures you're gonna kill somebody or something."

"Yeah?"

"Yeah. Well, so they're sendin' you to LBJ."

"They can't. I ain't been tried yet."

"It's called pre-trial confinement. They don't want you here."

Lopez loaded his pipe and lit it. He offered it to Blooms.

"No. Pre-trial confinement? Oh well, I wasn't havin' no fun here anyway. LBJ?"

Lopez nodded.

"Well, I guess I won't have ta haul ammo after all. Vacation."

"Yeah, I guess. How you feel about it?"

"I been in jail before. Won't be the last time either. Ain't much goin' on here, except maybe a chance to get killed."

"I guess, but the stockade's bad time, you know. It doesn't go toward time in service."

"I don't care."

Lopez leaned back and drew on his pipe.

"Well, listen to this, then, asshole. Guess who'n hell's takin' you to LBJ, and when?"

Blooms shrugged his shoulders.

Lopez leaned forward. "Me, that's who."

Blooms laughed, stared at Lopez, laughed again, pawed his swollen eyes. "Oh yeah?"

Lopez nodded.

"When?"

"This morning, zero five-thirty or so, on the slick."

Blooms looked at him for a moment, then blinked. "Damn."

The guns quit just before dawn and the silence woke Lopez, who was dreaming about his Montagnard girlfriend and her family. He stood in the clearing of a teakwood forest just before dawn. Happily, he watched his girlfriend's father and his elephant, Swan. They hauled out bolt after bolt of teakwood, setting them in piles next to him in the clearing. His girlfriend ran in and out of the woods waving a native scarf made of cotton, with red, yellow, blue, white and green stripes. She sang, "How Much Is That Doggy in the Window?" She didn't know the meaning of the words, but after every verse, she ran up to him, slipped her hand down his pants, and kissed him.

Swan kept hauling teakwood, dropping the bolts in the red dust with loud booms. Just as the fire mission ended, Swan dropped the last log, and he woke up. He got up and stretched.

Blooms woke up when he heard the joints crack in Lopez's body.

"I don't feel so hot."

"No wonder, asshole, the way you behaved last night."

"What time is it?"

"Soon to go, Wiley. Seems we do a lot of travelin' together. First one unit to another, now off to Saigon and LBJ."

"Saigon? I figured you'd try to get in a trip to Saigon. You gonna try? Even havin' to guard me too?"

"Well, why not? And if not Saigon, maybe Nha Trang. I know there's a flight to Nha Trang every mornin' out of Dalat. Maybe we'll take that route. I mean, as long as they're sending' us away, we might as well have some fun before you go to LBJ and I have to come back."

"You have the fun, Oscar. I'll watch. I'm broke."

"No sweat man. I owe you some bucks, and if we do get to Nha Trang, I can make some money."

"Know somethin', Oscar? You're a hell of a lot different than when you was new in country. You was scared of your own shadow back then. Now? Reckless."

"Reckless? Don't talk to me about bein' reckless, Blooms, not so soon after last night. The first sergeant just about went nuts!" Lopez laughed and stood up.

But he stopped short when he felt the weight in his cargo pants.

"Oh yeah, I forgot to tell you about somethin' last night, Wiley."

Blooms tilted his head up from where he sat and looked obliquely at Lopez.

He pulled out the pistol. Blooms did not react, and it was quiet in the room.

Finally Blooms spoke. "What's that?"

"Are you crazy? What the hell d'ya think is it?"

"Well, I mean, what are you doin' with it?"

"Smoke gave it to me."

"Smoke?"

Lopez nodded. "Come on, we gotta get goin' before the chopper gets here."

They climbed out of the hootch and headed across the firebase. The sun was up, and it lit the hilltops, and the houses, stores, and tin roof shacks of the hamlet beyond the firebase. Lopez and Blooms scurried through the red dust, observing women as they came from their homes to begin their day, wearing conical hats and ao dai skirts. They looked fresh, even in the distance. But the men, some of them troops in the army of the Republic of Vietnam, and some of them civilians, looked rumpled, still sleep-logged, as they drove their small, two-cycle motorcycles through the morning haze. From where Lopez and Blooms observed, they could not hear the motors, and it appeared as a provincial pantomime, all well-ordered and directed, the plot of which, although simple, perhaps, remained too far reaching for any one person to comprehend.

"Nice mornin' wouldn't you think?"

"Where we headed Oscar?"

Lopez pointed to gun pit two and then hopped up and over the sandbags and down into the pit. Then they dispersed, each addressing particular friends or associates. The crew continued cleaning the howitzer and throwing away empty ammunition boxes or collecting spent brass.

"Have a nice night, boys?" Lopez asked as he strutted through the pit.

"There it is, Oscar. What you got goin' on this early in the morning?"

"Where's Reynolds?"

A gunner stood up from where he was disassembling the breechblock. "Oh, Lopez, want your money, or something?"

Lopes shrugged. "Well, you know how it is. If you don't have it all I can wait on some of it. I can't expect all my debts paid in full."

Reynolds smiled. "Ah, you're a gentleman, Oscar. As a matter of fact, I can get you most of it right now."

"Good!"

"What's up? Why do you need the money so early in the day?"

Lopez pointed at Blooms, who was talking to a group on the other side of the pit. "Wiley and me are goin' to town and we need some bucks. I'm workin' on a deal, if we can get to Nha Trang. I figure our travel orders will send us through Nha Trang, you see, and . . ."

"Don't want to hear about it, Oscar. But if you score . . ."

"Right, I know."

"Okay, will MPC do? That's all I got. I don't have gook money."

Lopez agreed and Reynolds pulled out a wad of military pay certificates.

"Thanks, see ya." He turned to Blooms, who was shaking hands with somebody. "Hey, Blooms, let's go!"

Blooms sauntered over to Lopez. "I was sayin' goodbye to old Hector. Him and you the only friends I ever had in this fucked-up unit. Ain't never comin' back, probably."

They scurried out of the pit and headed for another gun crew.

"How much do I owe you, Wiley?"

"Eighty, I guess."

Lopez handed him some of the bills. "So much for that."

"That was fast, Oscar, where'd you get it?"

"From a friend. It was easy, but the rest is gonna be hard."

"Oh? Why? You talking 'bout that deal you had with Washington?"

"Yeah. You do remember Washington, don't you? Well, when he split, he had a lot of my money, for a deal we were makin'. And I think he sent the money back to his old section when he finally realized he wasn't comin' back, but section six ain't too honest."

"Where d'ya suppose he ended up anyway?"

"Don't really know, but he introduced me to a dude in Nha Trang, some old English fart that's been here since the Japanese or something. Maybe he took up with him. Maybe, if we make it to Nha Trang, we'll find him. I don't know. All I know is I'm gonna try to score some bucks off section six."

They dropped into section six's gun pit.

"Mornin' gentlemen, have a good night?"

The crew was just about finished maintaining the gun, and they all stopped to stare at Lopez and Blooms. A big, black, section chief stepped up to Lopez.

"We heard 'bout Blooms here last night. And we heard 'bout you escorting him to LBJ this mornin', too." He turned to look at his crew, then back to Lopez. "So why you here?"

They stared at each other, not smiling, expressionless, then Lopez put on a syrupy grin.

"Come on now, Linus, what you bein' so hard assed for?"

"'Cause I know you, Oscar. And I know you wanna make a deal when you is off the firebase. Well, that's fine. I hope you makes your deal. But I hope you don't think jest 'cause Washington owes you, and jest 'cause he used to be in this section, that you gonna get money from us. 'cause you ain't!" His crew roared its approval.

"Now look, fellahs . . ." Lopez raise his voice so they could hear him over their laughing. "That's just not the case. There's more to it." He put his arm around the section chief's shoulder. "How 'bout if we go down in your hootch where it's cooler, and have a bowl and talk it over?"

"It ain't hot yet, Oscar."

"Okay, I know, but why don't you take a break anyway?"

The section chief put his hands on his hips and rocked from toe to heel. Finally, he turned to the howitzer, then his crew. Then, in a low voice, he spoke. "Okay, let's take a break." The crew, followed by Lopez and Blooms, filed down into the hootch and sat in a big room around their poker table. By the time they were all settled, three pipes of marijuana were passed around.

Lopez breathed deeply, released, crossed his legs, rested his hands behind his head, and leaned back against the wall. He looked over at Blooms, then at the crew.

"For the time being," he began, "let's forget about any of my money that I think you might have."

Blooms listened to Lopez as he unraveled his story of how they met. He did not know exactly why Lopez was getting into such a complicated issue. They would be leaving soon, and he would probably never see these men again, except maybe at his trial. It seemed as if Lopez was just wasting time, Blooms thought. He heard Lopez talking about himself when he was new in country. Everyone called him, and everyone else that had just arrived, a 'cherry boy'. He remembered Lopez as he appeared eight months earlier, with clean campaign togs; exhibiting a sick expression that came from the slight case of dysentery that everyone had to suffer for the first week or so. It was also a sick expression that resulted from not knowing what was happening, and despair, and maybe loneliness. That was what affected Blooms. Lopez's sick loneliness. It seemed deeper than normal, or perhaps

Lopez was more sensitive. Blooms did not know, but he felt like befriending Lopez, maybe so that he, Blooms, might not be so lonely. He listened to him ramble on.

Lopez changed the subject, or at least he was talking about Blooms now. He told about how they became closer friends. Blooms remembered the night. He was drunk. He started drinking in the afternoon that day, after mail call. It was a letter from home, from his younger sister, that paved the way for the alcohol. The letter told him more news about his dead brother, Roland. It did not hurt that Roland was dead. Not too much. It was the way that he died, run over on the reservation blacktop, and the way his death was treated. Way within himself, he knew that he drank out of weakness, or some sort of disease, maybe. He didn't care about the cause. Let the experts and the eggheads worry about that. All he knew was that the last few times he drank heavy, it was out of despair that had something to do with Roland. Dead Roland.

Lopez carried on about how Blooms was on top of the fire direction control bunker, drinking and shooting off clip after clip of M-16 rounds. An infantry company had pulled in for the night, and they were on the verge of, as Lopez put it, "shootin' his ass off the bunker." The battery commander was running around the firebase informing everyone, "that son-of-a-bitch's got the whole damn firebase pinned down. No one can get into FDC, or out. Everyone's afraid of getting picked off by that sniper-crazy Indian." Hell, Blooms thought to himself, I was so drunk I couldn't hit the ground in front of me. I thought I was perched on the top of my own hootch. I guess I didn't really know where I was. "But Blooms didn't know where the hell he was," Lopez went on, "he could have been in Oklahoma for all he knew. In a way, it was sort of funny. I mean here we had one drunk fool, who didn't know what the hell was happenin' who was holdin' down the whole damn firing battery." Lopez looked around the poker table and here and there a smile began to bend away from flat, noncommittal lips.

But you're the crazy one, Oscar, Blooms recalled. You crawled up there behind me on the bunker and hauled me off before I really did get my ass shot. "You see, Blooms was the only guy I knew in the battery. We bunked together. He sold me marijuana. Hell he gave me more 'n I ever bought. And a lot of times he's smoke dope with me instead of gettin' shit-faced on beer. So when I saw him up there on FDC . . ." Lopez weaved his story, Blooms began to realize, in a way that put blame, or guilt, on Lopez's shoulders, not his. I guess he wants them to feel bad for me because we're good buddies and now he has to take me to jail. I wonder how much money they'll give him for feeling sorry.

Lopez took another draw on the pipe as it passed. He held in the smoke, pulling it in deeply, then exhaled in a long smooth passage. "So now I got stuck with this 'cause I guess they figure we're friends. You know, been in two units together. The BC would just a soon get me out of here for a while, one less pothead to look at. I think they figure the worst thing that can happen is if I do what I'm told, and the best thing is maybe we'll end up killin' each other." He hauled out the pistol. "Look, they even gave me the piece to do it." He handed the pistol to the section chief.

He cleared his throat. "What I'm lookin' for . . . is for you to lend us some bucks, so we can have a good time. It's just a loan. We wanna have a good time, just like you would, too."

The section chief returned the pistol to Lopez. He looked all around the poker table at his crew. Then he turned to Lopez and Blooms. "Wait outside."

They went outside and stood around in the gun pit.

"Ah, Wiley, I hated sayin' all those things in there 'bout you. It's none of their business."

"What you sorry for? You probably saved my ass. Now that I'm leavin' here I don't care what they know. When we leave on that chopper, that's it for me, no memories."

"Well, I'm sorry anyway."

"You got this thing 'bout bein' sorry, Oscar. I don't understand it. Seems like all the time you're sorry, or you want somebody else to be sorry. You gotta quit bein' sorry, man."

"I know. There's a lot to be sorry about."

"Forget about it, Oscar. Just forget it."

"Can you?"

"No."

"Well, at least you're honest. I'm workin' on it. Someday I'll do somethin' I won't be sorry for."

"There it is," Blooms replied.

They heard footsteps on the stairs of the hootch. It was the section chief, followed by some of the crew.

"Well, Linus?"

"We ain't terrible concerned 'bout you, Oscar," he replied. Then he faced Blooms. "But we figure long as you goin' to jail, Wiley, you might as well have some fun along the way. We took up a collection. Here, take it." He handed Blooms a roll of MPC. "One hundred fifty dollars for a good troop, deserves better 'n LBJ. If only you'd quit shootin' off your rifle."

Blooms lowered his head and took the roll.

The section chief continued. "Now, when you leavin?"

"In about fifteen minutes or so, as soon as the slick gets here."

"Well, let's all go back downstairs and have a farewell get together. You too, Oscar, come on now."

"Much obliged, Linus, but I have some more business. Besides, I'll be back at the firebase in a few days. We got a lot of partyin' to do before I get out of here.

"Wiley? Give me about fifteen bucks or so. I got to pay Lili before we go."

"You're payin' your hootch maid fifteen bucks?" Wiley asked.

"Yeah, I'm a sucker, I guess. She's got her family to support. Anyway, I'll be back in five minutes, then we gotta be at the LZ early to get our travel orders. Don't start playin' poker with these dudes, they'll strip you clean in ten minutes."

Lopez departed, and the little group laughed and ambled down the stairs and into the hootch.

"Numbah ten, Oska." Lili pointed her large whisk broom at the scorpion she had just crushed on the floor of his room.

"Oh! You okay, Lili?"

"No sweat, man, I got big broom."

"Good, good." He stuffed his hands in his pockets and paced around while humming his girlfriend's favorite tune. Lili, who had begun sweeping again, stopped, and cocked an upward eye at him.

"You beaucoup deeky-dow, man. What you do?"

"Guess what, Lili?"

"I no can guess. I clean room, you tell."

"Aw, come on, take a guess."

She stopped sweeping but kept her eyes on the floor. "You go home?"

"Naw. I'm goin' to LBJ, and Saigon, and maybe Nha Trang. Just found out last night."

"Why you go LBJ?" She stroked tentatively at the dirt with her giant whisk broom.

"I'm takin' Wiley Blooms to jail. He made a number ten mistake last night."

"Oh, he make beaucoup loud noise and go shoot, shoot?" She used her broom to illustrate the shooting.

"There it is. You hear it?"

"I hear. Get scared."

"Me too!"

She giggled, then touched his sleeve. "Why he do?"

"Oh, he got drunk and shot up ammo section. Then he came out to talk to me and got rowdy. That's when the Claymore went off."

"He beaucoup drunk?" She swept around the scorpion, whose stinger still convulsed. Then she sat on his couch while he stuffed provisions in his backpack. "Numbah ten, man."

"Who, Wiley?"

She nodded.

"Come on, Lili, give him a break. We're all a long way from home. Or are you mad at him 'cause he's an Indian? Is that it?"

He took her hands and helped her up.

"It seems a lot of Vietnamese don't like Indians, or blacks. Why is that, Lili?"

"They numbah ten, man. Mama-san, she say they numbah ten."

"I see. Looks like you're learnin' the secret lessens of humanity already."

He dropped her hands and took the holster and pistol out of his pants cargo pocket.

Lili move away. "Why you have?"

"This? I'm supposed to use it on the Indian if he makes a false move."

"He try to, to . . ."

"To escape?"

She nodded.

"I don't know. I guess I don't care." He reached under his cot and pulled out an ammunition can. She looked on curiously while he took the clips out of his shirt cargo pocket and put them in the can. Then he shoved the can underneath the cot.

"You no take bullets?"

"There it is, Lili. We're friends. The way things are, I wouldn't shoot him. Understand?"

"You beaucoup deeky-dow."

"Yeah, I suppose I am crazy. So what? Well, I gotta go now, minoi, my number one hootch maid. Here's an advance." She took the fifteen dollars. "Knock yourself out. Don't get in trouble with your boyfriend, okay?" He ducked out.

She yelled something after him in Vietnamese and bounced her broom off his backside as he left. But he just laughed, and she laughed with him. Then she caught sight of the scorpion and caught her breath in a short, laughter stopping way.

Lopez giggled to himself as he left the hootch. People, he thought to himself, people sure make things confusing. Lili sure is a sweet little thing, but just because mama-san says a guy's number ten, she won't see his good points. Maybe if I cut her wages until she likes Blooms she'd come around. No, why make her a hypocrite? He was ready to pick up Blooms when he felt the concussion from the blades of the arriving helicopter. Then he heard it. It would be on the landing zone within a minute, and he knew he had to get Blooms before they were missed.

Blooms stood on the second step of the hootch. He waved to Lopez and they watched as the helicopter touched once, then again, and came to rest on the pad.

"Have everything you need, Wiley? We can get some stuff down in Dalat if you want."

"Nah. Let's just get out a' here. Look, there's Top and the XO."

The first sergeant and executive officer stood on the edge of the landing zone, holding their caps on in the wind from the helicopter. Red dust swirled around them, partly obscuring them from view. They all waited for the blades to stop, then Lopez and Blooms moved up to them.

"Good morning, Top."

"Lopez, where the hell have you been?"

"Well, Top, I had to collect on some old debts and get ready and stuff. You know."

"Never mind, Lopez."

The gunner in the helicopter motioned for them to hurry up.

"Okay, here are your travel orders. And these are Blooms's special orders. Now listen up." The first sergeant cleared his throat. "Now this slick will only take you as far as the air strip. Your orders will get you a boarding pass for Nha Trang. From Nha Trang, you get passes to Ton Son Nhut. That understood?"

Lopez smiled. "Oh sure, I understand."

"Okay, when you get to Ton Son Nhut, get a military bus to Long Binh. If it's too late, stay at Camp Alpha, then go in the morning. You make it to Camp Alpha by this evening, and I don't want to hear about any trips to Saigon."

"Right, forget Saigon."

"I want Blooms delivered by tomorrow afternoon at the latest. And I want you back here in forty-eight hours."

Lopez nodded.

"Blooms, Lopez is armed and ordered to shoot if necessary. Is that understood?"

Blooms smiled and said he understood.

"All right then, I've wasted enough time on you. Now get out."

The helicopter crew was taking on battalion personnel while the first sergeant spoke, and they had just settled into the hold when Lopez and Blooms boarded. They took seats next to the cockpit and strapped themselves in. The gunner swung the machine gun into position. They all peered out the cargo hold to see the XO signaling for them to take off. The motor whined. The blades whipped the air, slowly at first, making a thumping sound as each blade swung past the open hold. Soon the thumping sound rocked the helicopter. Then, with a jolt, the helicopter flexed into the air and banked. Everyone in the hold instinctively grabbed something bolted down and they felt their stomachs rise as the land fell away down the face of the hill. The countryside raced by in blurs of green, dotted with reds and yellows throughout the terrain.

They churned down the middle of the valley, five hundred feet off the valley floor. Then the helicopter pitched dramatically, which swung them crazily from the waist up. By the time they settled back, they were a thousand feet off the floor of another valley, and already descending toward the airstrip. They caught sporadic glimpses of the strip as the helicopter swiveled in the wind. Within a few minutes it held itself over the landing pad at Dalat terminal. It bumped once and was down. Lopez and Blooms sat quietly, watching as the gunner locked his piece, and everyone waited for the blades to stop. The copilot yelled through the bulkhead to unload. The battalion aides, always silent around troops, such as the gunner, or Lopez and Blooms, dusted themselves off and headed for a jeep waiting for them outside the terminal.

By the time Lopez and Blooms reached the terminal, the helicopter was whipping its blades again. They watched, squinting through the red dust caused by the downdraft. In a moment, the helicopter was thumping its way down the valley at low altitude, on its way to some other firebase or terminal. Lopez and Blooms wandered into the sandbagged pole barn that served as Dalat terminal. They rubbed their eyes, watering them to shed the dust, and to adjust from the morning brightness to the dark bowels of the building.

"Dust or mud, that's all I'll remember about this place. You hungry, Wiley?"

"I don't know. Not much, I guess."

They found their way to the reservation desk. Lopez showed their orders to the airman on duty. He looked at the orders, then at Blooms, then Lopez.

"Plane leaves in ninety minutes, be here half an hour before departure."

"Thank you. What type of plane is it?"

"Probably a C-7A."

"Okay, one more thing, please, is that place across the street open this time of day?"

"What, the mission?"

"Yeah, I mean for food. Do they serve troops there and everything?"

"Sure, yeah, they're always open, someone's always there."

"Thanks, see ya later." Lopez turned to Blooms, winked and motioned for them to go.

The airman scratched his head as he watched them cross the street to the mission. He shook his head again, then yelled at the Vietnamese boy who was cleaning ashtrays. Another hot say in Vietnam had begun.

A young woman opened the front door to the mission. In a small, displaced voice she asked what they wanted.

"We'd like to eat, that is, if your kitchen's open."

She looked back into the house at a nun, partially hidden in the shadow of potted evergreen standing in the hall. The nun signaled with a slight motion of her hand, then walked away. The girl turned back to them. "We have a table ready in the veranda. Please come with me. It is early, but if you are hungry, then we will serve you."

She led them through a center hallway, past where the nun had stood, and all the way to the back of the house. Her sandals treaded on the hardwood floor in silence. Lopez's and Blooms's jungle boots clopped beneath them, leaving a layer of red dust over the wax. The floor's shaded calm seeped through the soles of their boots and the cool hallway air bloused their pants, making their legs ache in a light, not unpleasant way.

Lopez counted six potted ferns set along the baseboards, next to the windows. Several children, dressed in European fashion, trundled past them in makeshift formation. They balanced bushel baskets of fresh fruits and vegetables, suspended from cane poles that drooped over their shoulders in front and back. They giggled at the two soldiers, but stopped short when they heard the sharp clap of the nun's hands, who had returned to oversee their passage through the halls. But they giggled again as they turned the corner, and there was no clapping of the hands this time. The girl-san seated them next to the bay windows in the veranda that overlooked the mission's garden and stream.

The temperature in the valley was already in the nineties, but in the mission, Lopez and Blooms were almost chilled as they sat quietly in their sweat-soaked campaign togs. They were quiet in deference to the appointments around them, the clean floors and walls and ceilings, and the sparkling window glass. The sun highlighted their table, and then fanned into prismatic color on the crystal that rested on the shelves of the walnut server next to their table. A woolen tapestry, depicting Joan of Arc pleading with the king of France, hung on the wall behind them. It puffed and rippled whenever a door, in some other quarter of the mansion-like home, was opened or shut.

They heard a tinkling sound and turned to watch the girl-san glide to a stop in front of them. She filled their glasses with ice water from a pitcher and waited for them to order.

"Do you have taco burritos?" Lopez asked.

Blooms laughed at the improbability and because Lopez was not even Hispanic.

"We only have what is on the menu."

Lopez looked at the menu. "Well, I don't understand Vietnamese or French, but this is what I'll have. He stroked, and then chewed on his mustache. "First, some soup or salad, then a filet mignon, rare, baked potato with sour cream, green beans, and some sort of French pastry. Okay?"

She nodded, then turned to Blooms.

"Sounds good. I'll have the same. Thanks."

The girl-san made a few scribbles on her piece of paper, then left.

Blooms leaned over the table. "Do they really have all that stuff here? I'd settle for a taco burrito."

"Hey, this place is first class, even if it's a mission. The church's got all the people with money on their side." Lopez took a long drink of water, then set the glass softly on the same water ring on the linen tablecloth. "If you're worried 'bout what it costs, forget it. It's on me."

(Continued on page 119)

Wiley

you take the travel orders
you take Wiley to Long Binh Jail for getting drunk, one
last time
at Da Lat you wait for a flight
an ARVN major says he's flying to Na Trang
he has room in his plane
you climb aboard
you sit in back
Wiley sits in the copilot's seat
the rice paddies shimmer below
puffy white clouds drift in a cobalt sky
the major asks Wiley, "You fly?"

(Continued on page 181)

"On you? Why?"

"Well, it's the least I can do for you, since I'm the one who is haulin' your ass to jail."

"Don't worry about it, Oscar. Someone's got to do it. I'm glad someone I know's escortin' me there. Besides, ain't you always sayin' you want to send some money home? Why spend it all on me?"

"Just forget it, okay? I feel bad enough the way it is. I don't wanna see you in jail, let alone be the one takin' you there. And if you feel like tryin' to get away, be my guest. I won't stop you."

Blooms laughed. "You're crazy, Oscar, really. You think they'd believe you if you told them I got away from you? They probably figure that's what we'd try to pull off, then hang both our asses."

They relaxed for a while, enjoying the stillness of the veranda, and the isolation from the Vietnam they knew best.

"This is nice," Blooms continued a bit later, "it's nice gettin' over on the army for a change."

"What do you mean?"

"Well, here we are, drawing combat pay for sittin' in this nice place, eatin' good food and bein' waited on. It's about time I got somethin' other than the usual from the army."

"You'll pay, Wiley, don't worry. You're goin' to LBJ tomorrow."

"I don't care."

"What you gonna do there?"

"How should I know? Have a lot of time to think about things."

The girl-san brought their soup and salad, and they hunched over their food, reverting to mess hall behavior.

The shoveled in their food as if the house was about to be shelled or overrun. Lopez realized how they were acting, and he saw the girl-san staring at them from behind the corner.

"Hey Wiley, what the hell we eatin' so fast for? Anyway, I thought you said you weren't hungry." He laughed.

Blooms mumbled through a mouthful of egg-drop soup. "Changed my mind." But he sat up, put his porcelain soup spoon down, and took a few deep breaths. "You're right, Oscar. It's time to eat slow for a change."

The girl-san returned with the meat and side dishes and took away the empty soup and salad bowls. They gawked at the meal that lay before them. They looked up, at each other, shook their heads and laughed quietly. Somehow, they sensed that they had won a small battle in this war they could not understand. The meal carried on and on, with the girl-san refilling their vegetable bowls with freshly picked and steamed green beans from the garden below and bringing them each another baked potato with more sour cream. Finally, they had to tell the girl-san to quit bringing any more food. It took a while to get her to understand, but then her face brightened and she smiled and nodded her head.

"I don't know about you, but I'm going out on the balcony and belch. I'm stuffed. I must have gained ten pounds." Lopez stood up and groped out the French doors to the balcony. Blooms joined him.

They stood side by side, belching and looking down into the garden that stretched before them on terraced sections with a stream that ran through it. A Montagnard woman worked in the bean patch, weeding, and opening irrigations dams, then closing them again.

"Well," Lopez said, "I'm gonna pay the bill, then go check on our flight, just in case. Why don't you hang around and watch our packs, okay, Wiley?"

Blooms sat down, resting his elbows on the balcony railing. Not looking at Lopez, he nodded, and Lopez was gone. He sat as still as he could, examining the neatly designed and maintained garden. He tried to identify the fruits and vegetables, shrubs and trees, flowers and herbs and spices that he saw spread before him. All he could get through were the beans and potatoes, and possibly catnip. Potatoes in Vietnam? He wondered. His eyes were drawn to the glinting water as it ran through the stream and its irrigation ditches. He listened to its endless, lyrical message. Then he heard, ever so slightly, the Montagnard woman humming as she worked through another section of beans, weeding them on her hands and knees. She wore the customary dress of her tribe, a blanket wrapped around her to her knees, tied at her tiny but sturdy waist, and left a little open on top. Her skin, a luminous bronze, glowed beneath the bright colors of her blanket and her hair was dark brown with blond bands in it from working under the sun all her life. Unlike the Vietnamese, which her tribe disliked and did not trust, her hair was wavy to the point of almost being out of control. But it was controlled, and it reminded Blooms of the music he heard in the stream that ran next to her.

The garden and the woman, although unlike anything Blooms knew of his life before Vietnam, reminded him of home. His sensibilities were soothed with the scene before him, and as he relaxed, digesting his excellent and recent meal, he began thinking of home, and he knew that this way of thinking of home would maybe be different from the way he generally remembered it. He would go for weeks without thinking of home. His family, his friends, would all vanish from his life, then his grandmother would recall him. Somehow she could reach him. Maybe she did not even know it, but she could reach him.

He almost smiled, and just then the quality of his thought altered, and a cloud came over his face. He clenched his fists, and his breathing went shallow and quick. "Roland!" He hissed.

"What's that?" It was Lopez.

Blooms snapped his head back toward Lopez and burned through him with his eyes. "Nuthin'!"

Lopez stopped short and frowned at Blooms for an instant. He ignored the fists, which were still clinched, and the breathing which, though deepening, was still too quick.

"Come on, Wiley, we got a change in plans."

"What's that?"

"I said come on, we gotta go, right now."

"Oh, the plane got here early?"

"No, Wiley, but our karma has just changed."

"Oh shut up, Lopez. You been smokin' again?"

"Well, yeah, I had a bowl."

With Lopez's urging, they hustled out of the mission, across the street, through the terminal, and out onto the taxi apron.

"There," said Lopez, "you see that single engine job down there? It's the last one on the line. That's our ride. What dy'a think of that?"

Blooms squinted down the apron, shading his eyes from the sun. He took a deep breath and faced Lopez. "I think you should get that idiot grin off your face. Reminds me of the first time you got laid over here." He focused on the plane again. "Sure is a small sucker. Looks like a man and a boy are standin' there with it. Who are they?"

"That's the guy who's gonna fly us to Nha Trang. Says he's a major in the Vietnam air force. Jeeze, I didn't know they even had an air force. And that's his kid with 'em."

"Are you serious? You're god damn serious! I ain't flyin' with no . . ."

"Look, Wiley, I checked it out and . . ."

"Oh, you checked it out?"

"Yes, and this guy's for real. So . . ."

"So you didn't check it out with me."

Lopez stopped and flashed his idiot grin at Blooms again. "I seem to recall that you are my prisoner." He put his arm around Blooms. "Hey look, I'm just kiddin' about that. Anyway, I was checking on our flight when this major comes up to the airman and asks if there's anyone ticketed for Nha Trang. The agent points to me and says I have two boarding passes for Nha Trang. Then this guy asks if I want to go with him in his own plane and he points to it settin' out there on the runway." He caught his breath and got them moving again. "And I say 'sure' and he says 'Okay. we leave in ten minutes.' And that's when I came to get you. See?"

"Why's he givin' a couple gun bunnies like us a ride? I don't like it. How d'ya know we ain't gonna end up in North Vietnam or something? Anyway, that guy don't look like he could fly a kite."

"Well, let's just ask him why and if it don't sound good, we'll just wait for the plane. Come on, Wiley, give it a chance."

They were nearing the light plane and Blooms frowned at the major, who stood leaning against the open passenger-side door. Lopez smiled at the major and he smiled back.

"You are on time. Are you ready?"

"Ah, well, you see, major, my friend here, Wiley Blooms, doesn't quite understand why you want to fly us to Nha Trang."

"Yes, of course. I understand. First of all, this is my son, he will be flying with us."

He turned to the boy and rattled off something in Vietnamese and the boy climbed into the back seat and buckled himself in. Then the major smiled broadly at Lopez and Blooms. "You realize, of course, that I would be flying to Nha Trang even if you two do not come along?"

Lopez and Blooms nodded to each other, cocking their heads and pushing out their bottom lips.

"The reason I ask for passengers then, is to make it a more economic flight."

"Well, why should you be so economic when most pilots never give enlisted guys a lift?"

"Yes," the major replied, "it is personal decision I have made. You see, your government gives me the uses of this plane. I must make better uses of it if I can. So, we must go now. Please?" He motioned for them to board the plane.

"Sounds good to me. How 'bout you, Wiley?"

Blooms scanned the observation plane, tapping on the wing. Without facing either of them he replied. "Do you know what would happen if this little fart ever went down? If we didn't turn up crispy critters, the Cong would march us straight to North Vietnam."

"That'd happen if we were in any plane, Wiley."

"I'd rather take my chances in a C-7A."

"Oh?" Lopez tapped him on the shoulder, and then pointed to a jackknifed, burned and gutted C-7A that lay abandoned on the edge of the runway.

Blooms shrugged his shoulders, took another glance at the observation plane, then peeked at the C-7A out of the corner of his eye. "Nuthin's bad as it seems," he muttered, "unless it's worse."

"I guess that means you'll go . . ."

"Please, now we must go," the major politely interrupted. He motioned for Lopez to climb in back with his son. Then he gave the plane a final, overall inspection, and boarded through the pilot-side door, leaving Blooms standing under the wing.

Lopez stuck his head out. "Come on, Wiley! The major's a busy man." He pointed at the major, who was strapping himself in. "Let's go, get in and close the door, Wiley." He turned to the major, who seemed to be thinking twice about his offer. "Ah, you see, major, my friend's a little worried 'bout flying. Thinks we'll crash or something." The major frowned at the word crash. "No, forget about crash, or, I mean, jeese . . . you see, sir, he's just upset." Lopez stuck his head out and whispered, "Wiley, will you get your fuckin' ass in this plane?"

Blooms sighed. Then he climbed into the copilot's seat and slammed the door. It didn't latch and Blooms sighed. He gave it another slam and it latched.

The major made some last-minute adjustments. He pulled on a knob and pushed a button. There was a whirring noise and the propeller turned. The little motor caught, coughing and belching white smoke. It smoothed out some, and steadied into a vibration that ran up their backs and ended in the back of their heads. They were strapped in and the major waited for the tiny plane to build its nerve. As the revolutions built, the whole thing began to shake. The plexiglass windows rattled, and it seemed like all the bolts in the cabin were coming loose. Blooms let out with a quite audible sigh. The major shouted something in Vietnamese into the microphone. Something in Vietnamese came back over the speaker. He taxied the little affair out onto the runway and headed them down the linked metal surface of the runway. Oil from the motor spattered on the windshield as they gained speed and the major waggled the rudder once, slightly, pulled back on the wheel, and their wheels left the ground.

When they gained altitude, they banked left over the sparse, shrapnel-riddled trees that stood on the crest of the hills. Blooms saw three smudgy fires along the ridge tops. Gathered around the fires stood small groups of Montagnard men and boys who were melting down discarded communication wire for the copper. Then the valley wall raced up the hills and the major slung the little plane through a wide, low pass, heading them for Nha Trang.

The cloud-mottled sky offered little resistance to the plane. Occasionally a wing tip would flutter as they passed near some innocuous looking cloud, or the high-spirited little motor would catch for about a tenth of a second, also stopping Blooms's heart for as long. But he had ceased sighing, and when he turned back to see Lopez, he would still be wearing that idiot grin that had infuriated most of his superiors, but endeared him to his pot head friends. So Blooms relaxed some, and thoughts of home seeped back back into the low spots of his consciousness. Roland, he thought to himself. Lopez heard me say his name in the mission but he ignored it. I love him for that. He's the only one on this side of the earth, besides me, that knows anything about Roland. Roland who is dead. Who is killed and who bleeds on the reservation blacktop on a Saturday night. Whose body is battered into a final, bloody death.

He caught a glimpse of the jungle below. Man, check out all the jungly looking stuff down there. Rice paddies too, miles and miles of it. I wish Roland could see this, and my sisters. He'd like all this. My sisters would only giggle, but Roland, he'd make this work in his own world. Poor sucker, he was too gone even for the reservation. Grandmother used to say his kind never lived in time, only space. He reminded her of her great-uncle who wondered away when she was seven. The never found him. But they found my brother. Blooms thought, stuck on the reservation blacktop, stuck in his own blood. My blood.

They approached a pattern of pillow-like clouds, and he remembered lying on the prairie, in the tall grass beneath the wind with his grandmother. They watched the clouds, then. They rushed by in silent tribes while she stitched the generations together with her lore, and with her own crazy and meaningless stories that he could still remember. They had no endings, and he still continued to live out endings for them. He felt that he was living out an ending now, as they were flying over Vietnam, as he thought about Roland.

The plane bumped, and the right wing dipped below the horizon. The major explained that they were now on the coastal plane. Blooms noticed that the huge, rough hills had diminished to foothills, and now the foothills leveled to the coastal plane. The South China Sea opened on the horizon, blue, and indifferent. Soon they raised the harbor at Nha Trang which meandered below them toward the open sea. A brilliant, white thread of beach separated the land and water. They circled over the harbor, over wrecks, patrol boats, an Australian destroyer, junks, and endless sampans, and then swung back toward the airfield, which dealt out and received private planes, cargo planes, and F4 Phantoms. Below them the aircraft appeared as various size bugs, silver, black or olive drab. The major said something in Vietnamese over the microphone, then turned back to his son and said something in Vietnamese to him. In a moment someone was saying something in Vietnamese over the speaker. He acknowledged, hung up his microphone, and banked the plane. Outside the plexiglass, the horizon rolled up like a window shade. Blooms felt his stomach rising and he took some deep breaths. Lopez uttered a quiet "Jesus Christ." As one, they saw the cement runway rushing in below and in front of the nose. The major pulled back on the wheel to bring the nose up some. The runway grew in size and clarity. Skid marks from ten thousand landings stood out on the cement, and they felt themselves dropping into their final approach. Before it seemed the major could react, they bumped, came off, touched down, and raced along the runway. The major cut back his motor and taxied them in between and around the big planes, toward what looked like a comfortable spot next to the small planes. The building next to the small planes was decked out in oriental trim, and all the signs were in Vietnamese script and calligraphy. Shakily, Lopez and Blooms crawled out of the pane and stood on the ground, numb and silent. They slung their backpacks and headed for the Vietnamese terminal.

The bay doors of the terminal were slung open and Vietnamese troops and civilians moved in and out. Lopez and Blooms wandered in and stopped short. Lopez held his nose. Blooms mouthed softly, "What in hell?"

The major, who followed them in, explained.

"Viet Cong prisoners, or some who have come over in what you call 'Open Arms' policy."

"Well, I'll be damned if I couldn't smell 'em before I could see 'em. Unplug your nose, Oscar, might as well get used to it."

"Must be fifty of those dudes," Lopez said. "Walking wounded and everything."

Their eyes grew accustomed to the dim light inside the building, where the collection of Vietnamese men sat. They wore nothing but breech clouts and each was handcuffed. Some also wore dirty bandages or slings for broken arms, and some displayed open wounds and sores. They barely moved, and remained absolutely quiet, like a group of captured animals, aware of nothing but their own fear. They smelled of the fermented jungle, musty, wet and pungent.

"They look like slaves or something," Lopez added. "Probably been in the bush for months, crawlin' through all those tunnels and everything." He stepped around a guard. "Looks like their friends here with the Sten guns have been persuading them to be friendly Chieu Hois. I always wondered about that open arms policy."

The guard watched Lopez and Blooms walk by. The major, who walked with them, spoke to the guards in Vietnamese and they immediately returned to watching over their prisoners.

"Some of these guys turned themselves in, right major?" Blooms asked. He wondered if he should tell the major that he himself was a prisoner.

"Yes, our ground troops are relentless." The major and his son stopped to look at a group of men who were trying to get the major's attention. "My son and I must go now to Cambodian compound. I suggest that you do not stay here. You are only Americans in terminal, and this makes guards nervous. They do not want you to see prisoners. It is a matter for the Vietnamese people. We have been at war for a long time. Good fortune of guards is bad fortune for prisoners, and everyone in this terminal, and everywhere else in our country, knows it would not take much for guards to be prisoners and prisoners the guards. It is simple matter of what you call fate. We do not like outsiders observing how fate is tearing our people apart." He motioned for his son to move on. "I thank you for filling plane your government has given our government. Perhaps, if all flights were full, even observations planes, your newspapers would not speak so often of waste."

The major and his son walked away. Lopez and Blooms left the shade of the building and headed toward the international gate. Neither of them spoke as they tried to adjust to the increasing heat. Lopez loaded his pipe and drew on it leisurely as they headed down the blacktop. In the distance a guard bunker and the international gate shimmered in the sink of heat waves. A long mirage coated the blacktop and a three-quarter ton truck labored through it, reflected off the road surface. Lopez resumed his girlfriend's favorite tune, humming off-key in an interrupted rhythm. Blooms slowed his pace in order to stay with Lopez. It was very hot, walking along the road with red dirt stretching out farther than the eye could see, with clusters of one-story buildings scattered here and there, and Nha Trang's outskirts close on hand. To take his mind off the heat, Blooms recollected the flight, the mission, the drinking and the shooting of the night before, and then, back into a miasma of events that were his past.

Lopez stopped humming. "Wiley. Is Roland the reason you lost it last night?"

"You never can say his name right."

"How do you say it? Do I say your name right?"

"You don't say it exactly wrong. It's a matter of tone quality. That was a big part of Roland's life. The quality of tones."

"What are you talking about?"

"His flute. Roland played a flute that he made himself. I never told you about that."

"But what's that got to do with you? I saw you back in the mission, Wiley. I've seen you like that before." He offered his pipe to Blooms.

"Sure." Blooms took a long drag and returned the pipe. "I get mad. That's all."

"That's enough."

"Well, I forget about everything back home for a long time. I mean everything. There is no home. I'm here, drifting, alone. Sometimes it lasts a month or more. When I remember, I get mad, or scared."

"I can dig it, Wiley. It happens to me too. It's scary. It's like, half the world just is gone. And when you remember it, it's just so meaningless, anything that can be forgotten so easy, or for so long. But then you think of the people. Do you think of the people, Wiley?"

"That's what brings me back. Someone reaches me. Grandmother." He turned to Lopez. "But it's different with you, isn't it, Oscar?" Lopez hung his head. "You don't have anyone to remind you that there's something else in the world besides this, do you?"

Lopez looked up. "I remember the world."

"What reminds you of it?"

"You."

"I wrote grandmother 'bout you. You remind me of Roland."

They were approaching that gate. Lopez got his papers ready in case anyone wanted to check. It was hotter now, and there was no traffic. The guards wanted to stay inside. One of them waved the two on through, exclaiming from within the bunker something that they took to be an insult. They ignored the guard as they strolled by.

"Roland?"

"Yeah?"

"Why?"

"'Cause you don't belong here."

"No one belongs here. This place should be paved with good U.S. cement and then forgotten."

"Roland didn't belong."

"Yeah, it's hard livin' there too."

"It's not some much the place, Oscar. It's the time. Roland lived in space, not time. That's what grandmother always said."

"How can you live in one and not the other?"

"It's hard. He didn't do so hot, toward the end."

"I know. You told me he's dead."

"Beat up, run over, left for the animals to clean up. They were on him when they found 'em."

They reached the main road to Nha Trang and stopped under the shade of a banana tree and shared the rest of Lopez's pipe as the traffic, light as it was, rolled by.

"And that's why you drink then, Wiley, and get your ass in a jam?"

"I drink, you smoke. What's the difference?"

"I don't know. Not all the information's in yet. But I don't get violent. You do."

"If I didn't drink, I'd kill myself."

"You are killing yourself."

"So are you."

"How?"

"By bein' sorry for things you can't help. Like for bein' in 'Nam. Like for takin' me to jail. Stuff like that. Don't be sorry."

"Was Roland sorry?"

"That's where you're different. He was never sorry. I learned not to be sorry from Roland. He learned it from grandmother. She learned it from her great-uncle."

"Where'd he learn it?"

Blooms turned and smiled at Lopez. "From the white man."

They sat down, leaning against the trunk of a tree, passing another pipe between them. After a long while, Lopez spoke.

"Why'd they kill him?"

"They were drunk."

"Who?"

"Cousins, I guess."

"They killed 'em 'cause they were drunk?"

"For them, it was a good enough reason."

"Why do you think they killed them?"

"They were afraid of Roland. He didn't drink. He played his flute all night long. He ignored them. He was better than them and they knew it. So they killed 'em." Blooms sank down a little more, pulled his boots in from when the sun crept from the shadow. "Roland and me, we used to ride our ponies out in the prairie when we was young. He was older and he knew a lot of places. We'd ride all day, never speakin' or anything. We'd just rest and he'd play his flute. He always had his flute. He died with his flute. They shoved it in his mouth, after they kicked his head in. That's what my sister said in her letter." Blooms drew designs in the red dirt with a twig. "And when we'd get off our ponies to rest, after we rode half the day, guess who's be out there? Alone, on foot?"

"I don't know."

"Grandmother."

"What was she doin' way out there?"

"Visitin' her great-uncle. That's what she'd say."

"All your relatives sound crazy, Wiley."

"Oh, you're right. All but me. And so that's why I'm the one that got sent to 'Nam. They don't send crazy people to 'Nam, do they Oscar?"

"Right, absolutely. They only send crazy people back to the World." Lopez stood up, wiping the red dust off his pants and scratching his head. "Hey, how did we get on this topic, anyway? This story just keeps goin' and there doesn't seem to be any point."

"That's just it, Oscar, there ain't no point. It just goes on and on."

"Well, we can't stay here all day, Wiley." He offered a hand to Blooms and pulled him up. "Let's get a ride to Nha Trang and get a place to stay for the night."

Soon they heard a Lambretta bouncing and rattling down the coastal highway. Lopez waved it down. "You go Nha Trang, papa-san?"

"I bek. I bek. One dollah, you pay now."

"Okay, papa-san. Here's a dollar, and here's a half dollar more. You go beaucoup slow, you bek?" He motioned his hand slowly and smoothly along the horizon leading to Nha Trang. "No bump-bump, slam-bang, okay?"

"You numbah one, GI. I go beaucoup slow. Where you go Nha Trang?"

"Nha Trang Hotel."

"Ah, numbah one! You get in. We go now."

Blooms hopped in back and Lopez tossed in their packs and jumped in after him. He smiled at Blooms across the narrow bed of the small, three-wheeled utility lorry.

"I was in Nha Trang once with Washington." He filled his pipe again, lit it and offered it to Blooms.

"I can't smoke as much marijuana as you, Oscar, no thanks."

"Yeah? Well anyway, we went and made a deal with this guy I told you about. He's got this place sort of close to the Nha Trang Hotel. Walking distance, you can see it from the top of the hotel roof. I think we should get rooms at the hotel and then I wanna visit this guy."

Blooms made a noncommittal move with his head and body, then squinted out of the rolled-up canvas sides of the Lambretta. Nha Trang grew in density. The women on the streets wore brightly colored ao dais and shopped or walked along the street markets. Children flicked in and out of store fronts, playing their games and practicing the stealth they would need to survive on the streets of a war city. Mama-sans and papa-sans squatted at selling stands or on street corners where the lottery was dealt. The old ones chewed betel nut and their teeth, if they had any, were red and rotted from years of the habit. They smoked unfiltered, unbranded cigarettes and turned their heads this way and that, observing everything and nothing in a single, mindless sweep, and wore coolie hats and squatted in the sun.

Fruits and vegetables squatted in the sun, too, and red and green and yellow banners flew from the street signs or second story balconies. A cobalt sky overarched the city, unaware that the city was ancient and sacred in the hearts of the Buddhist priests who displayed their moon-yellow robes and meditated on the city's bridges and public lawns.

And there were the shrieks and cries and celebrations and laments that flooded into the back of the Lambretta, where Lopez and Blooms bounced along engulfed within the tide of the city. Finally, the brakes of the little truck squeaked, and they were still, in the middle of the swell.

"Nha Trang Hotel!" papa-san yelled.

"Okay, papa-san, thanks for the ride."

They jumped out and Lopez inspected the hotel front. "Yeah, I remember that entrance across the street. It leads right upstairs to the bar on the roof. I can't believe we ain't there yet."

"Well, how 'bout a room first?" Blooms asked.

"Nah, let's just relax for a while. They always have rooms in the middle of the week."

They walked up the stairs and came out on the roof, five flights up. The stairs opened to a short hallway that led to a penthouse bar. The bar was empty except for a bar boy and several prostitutes lounging in their bed clothes at the far end of the bar. The boy-san was stocking the cooler behind the bar with beer and the piercing clinks he made when the bottles hit each other, punctuated the conversations of the ladies. They all turned to look at Lopez and Blooms when they entered. It was early yet for the ladies. Most of them had just gotten up for the day and none of them wore make up, and after the two troops sat down, they ignored them.

"What you have?" the boy-san asked.

"Well, let's see now," Lopez began. "What you have?"

"I got Bud, whiskey, gin, Coke."

"Great selection. Don't you have any Bhami-Bha?" Lopez held up three fingers, curled them over, then held them up again.

"You want Bhami-Bha? GI no like Bhami-Bha, why you drink?"

"He beaucoup deeky-dow, boy-san," Blooms interjected. "You got Bhami-Bha for deeky-down GI?"

"You want Bhami-Bha, I got."

"There it is. I'll have water." Blooms smiled at Lopez as they sat at the bar. "You're the only one I know besides me that'll drink that piss."

"I know. I picked it up from you. You're drinkin' water today?"

The boy-san brought over a dark brown, misshapen bottle of beer and a glass of water and Blooms peeled a dollar off his money roll and gave it to the boy-san. Before Lopez could take the bottle Blooms grabbed it and held it under his nose. Then he set it down and winked at him. "It's a good one." Then he drew his thumbnail through the paper label that had displayed a large, stylized thirty-three. "Yeah, my girlfriend told me once that if you're gonna drink this stuff you should smell every bottle and rip the label before you take a drink."

"Why?"

Blooms laughed. "I don't know, Oscar. I never thought to ask."

He finished his water in two long gulps. "Hell, I might as well get a room while you're doin' this. I really don't want to drink right now."

"I might be out on the patio when you get back, Wiley."

"How d'ya know I'll be back?"

Lopez shrugged his shoulders.

"I'll be back. Watch my pack."

Lopez nodded and Blooms went away. He finished his beer slowly and it helped him cool off from the Lambretta ride. The boy-san, who had finished stocking the cooler, stood behind the bar, smiling at Lopez whenever he looked at him.

"Let's have another beer, boy-san."

The boy-san brought the beer and took another dollar. He started to take a drink, then stopped and sniffed the mouth, and ripped the paper label. The prostitutes, who had been engaged in private conversation, laughed at Lopez when they saw him rip the label. He sat sideways to the bar on a swivel stool and watched the ladies as they talked among themselves. Some of them sat at the bar, and the rest were gathered at a table next to the bar. They trimmed their toenails and laughed together or held hands or picked lice out of each other's hair. One, who did more talking than the others, seemed upset at a girl who was younger than the others. The upset one pointed her finger at the younger one and waved it in front of her face while she uttered low, emotionally inflected threats. The young one stared back with calm, controlled silence. Finally, she batted the finger waver across the side of her head, but not with pain-inflicting force, issued her own series of threats and reprisals, and stormed past Lopez and out the door.

The group laughed and he laughed too. The upset one, who had been batted across the side of her head, saw him laughing and she pointed at him."

"Why you laugh, GI?"

He sat up, taking his elbow off the bar. He pointed at their end of the bar and clucked like a chicken. She unleashed a stream of Vietnamese at him, and he knew she was insulting him by the tone, and because the others were laughing again and encouraging her to go on.

"Aw, com'on, minoi, give me a break." He gave her an idiotic grin.

She stood up. "I not your minoi, GI. I not your honey."

"Well, can I buy you a beer?"

The prostitute machine gunned him with words, pointing here and there in his direction. He looked to where she was pointing, at his biceps, head, crotch, and laughed again. He was enjoying it. It was something female, he thought, and he missed it in the field. He laughed again, throwing his head back and draining his beer. The upset one continued until the bar boy interrupted with his own dress down of the prostitute. Then it was quiet again, and the bar boy and the prostitute engaged in a stare down. Finally, she gathered her things and ran out of the bar.

"Nuts!" Lopez said. "I didn't mean to upset anyone. Get me another Bhami-Bha, will you boy-san? And while you're at it why don't you treat the remaining ladies to whatever they like."

"They drink Coke," the boy-san said. "You buy Coke?"

"Not Saigon Tea?"

"Saigon Tea for night. Coke now. You buy?"

"Yeah. Tell 'em I'm not laughin' at them. I like them."

The boy-san beamed. "They know what you like, man."

Lopez burped and sat up straight. "I resent what you say, boy-san. I am an honorable troop."

"What you say?"

"Never mind."

The boy-san pulled out three cans of Coke and opened them, leaving them on the bar. The prostitutes watched the bar boy walk away, then an overweight one, with bleached and curled hair, got up and brought the Coke to where they sat.

"Four dollah, man. Three Coke, one beer."

Lopez gave him ten dollars in MPC.

"I no can change. I go see mama-san."

Lopez nodded and took his fresh beer out on the patio. Leave them in peace, he thought. Besides, I have some business out here.

On the patio, he stood by the railing and looked out over Nha Trang. "Where's the fish market?" He asked himself quietly, and then answered himself. "On a street that leads to the fish market." He followed along the distance of two streets until they came to a point. That did not work, so he located the fish market and traced back toward the hotel. After about two blocks he focused on a green, lacquered door, half a kilometer from the hotel. "Well now," he said under his breath.

But down at the desk, Blooms was not finding what he wanted.

"I want two rooms, mama-san, not one. You bek?"

"One GI, one room. Two GI, two room. I no see two GI."

"Look, mama-san, my buddy is upstairs drinkin' beer. Why do you care, anyway?"

"You want room? I got room. Three seventeen. Numbah one room, you like beaucoup. You pay fifteen dollah now, you stay twelve tomorrow."

"I want two rooms, mama-san, not one. You bek?"

"One GI, one room. Two GI, two room. I no see . . ."

"Yeah right, mama-san, okay, you win. Here." Blooms gave her some money. "Are you from Oklahoma City or something?"

The mama-san gave him his change and a key to room three seventeen. "No bek what you say. Why you say?"

"'cause it's about as hard to get what I want here as it is in Oklahoma City, that's why." He took his change and the key, and they stared at each other. "Well, we'll see ya, mama-san."

He climbed back up the stairs. Only the prostitutes were in the bar, but he saw the backpacks resting against the bar where they had been sitting. He looked around and saw Lopez out on the patio, with his hands shading his face, staring down into the city. He carried the packs out to the patio.

"You forgot these, Oscar. You must be slippin."

Lopez blinked at the packs. "Yeah, I suppose. D'ya get some rooms?"

"One."

"One? Why?"

"I was lucky to get one. Mama-san didn't want to rent to an Indian."

"How do you know that?"

"The eyes."

"Come on now, how . . ."

"It's a long story, Oscar, like the one about Roland and me and my grandmother. Forget it."

Lopez put his hand lightly on Blooms' shoulder. "All right. How much did she charge you then anyway?"

"Fifteen bucks, MPC."

"H'mmm, price's gone up since last time. What room?"

Blooms told him while Lopez loaded another pipe with marijuana. They stood together, next to the railing, sharing the pipe and watching the people in the fruit and meat market down on the street. The day had grown quite hot, and many of the stands in the market were closing, either because they had run out of goods and were leaving, or in preparation for a light nap when it grew too hot to do business.

"You told me what Roland was like, Wiley. What are your sisters like? Mind talkin' about that?"

"I don't mind talkin about anything, Oscar. It's just the explainin' part I don't like. You interested in my sisters?" Blooms smiled like the boy-san had smiled before.

"Not that way, Wiley. You got a letter from one of 'em yesterday. I know 'cause I tossed the letter on your cot while you were haulin' ammo."

Blooms dropped the smile, and he clenched his fist around the iron railing. His breathing became fast and shallow. Lopez offered him the pipe and he shook his head.

"The letter was a bummer?"

Blooms nodded.

"Wanna talk about it?" Lopez leaned on the railing with his elbow, facing Blooms, puffing on his pipe.

"You're actin' like a god damn counselor now, Lopez."

"I know I am, but it's your own damn fault."

"How?"

"I think probably the only reason we're here right now, with me actin' like a god damn counselor, is 'cause you got a letter from home that ticked you off. You got a case of the ass last night, and so now here we are."

Blooms reached in his cargo shirt pocket and pulled out an envelope. He passed it to Lopez. "Here, read it."

It was the letter he had dropped on Blooms' cot the day before.

Wiley Night Horse Blooms, I know you said you don't ever want to come home. We all know it since you didn't after Roland was killed. I can understand that I guess. I mean not coming home for Roland. You knew he was dead even before we did. Because you were so close. It's hard to tell you this Wiley. Your little sister is dead. The family is going to hell. She killed herself with her boyfriend's pistol. It took two shots. No one knows how she did it. But she's dead. No one knows what to do anymore. I thought I should write you instead of the Red Cross telling you. Will they let you come home? My friends say you can probably get a hardship discharge. Please Wiley, don't stay away from home if you can get out of there. I don't know what to say. Your sister wrote a poem the day she killed herself. I copied it for you to read.

> *Indian woman, empty womb*
> *Yanked bare by one*
> *white hand.*
> *Maybe the hand was red.*

> *Wiley, we are the only children left. Please come home.*
> *I don't know what to do.*

> *Alicia Night Horse Blooms*

Lopez gave him the letter.

"Did you show this to the BC, Wiley?"

He shook his head.

"Why not?"

Blooms looked at Lopez as if he had just discovered something about him that was ignorant and disgusting.

"Don't you want to go home?"

"How can I now? I'm goin' to jail."

"Well, tell someone about it. Show 'em the letter."

"I showed you."

"Well, I can't do anything about it."

"You're the only one who gives a shit, maybe."

"I don't understand any of this, Wiley. None of this seems to bother you. You're so quiet about it."

"Just because I'm quiet doesn't mean much. Besides, I tried to tell you somethin' last night and you and Nugent didn't take it too seriously, did you?"

"Well, that was different."

"It's always different."

"I'm sorry, Wiley. I didn't know."

"Don't be sorry, Oscar. You got your own life to live. So do the people left in my family. Alicia will find out what to do if I'm there or not. Right about now, all I have is what Roland taught me."

"What's that?"

"That the difference between life and death is only a heartbeat. That in life, the only thing that is real is the sureness of death, and that in death, the only thing that is real is the sureness of life."

"I don't understand what that has to do with the letter, or with what you did last night, or in our last unit, or what we're doin' right now."

Bloom signed. "There is no connection, I guess. All I know is that if I get started wondering about it, sometimes I feel cheated, and then I get to feelin' sorry, like last night, and drinkin' and gettin' mad at everything. It's a cycle. I have some control for a while, or it seems that way, but in the end, I get pushed with the flow and if I fight, like last night, well . . ."

"Yeah, I know, Wiley. It's like karma. It's what you got dealt, sort of, right there in the beginning, and you just do what you can, and try not to lose your cool."

They hooked thumbs, clasped hands. "There it is."

They watched the streets of the market for a while longer. Business had dwindled since the sun climbed so high in the sky.

"Let's get on the streets, Wiley. I spotted the little joint I should visit, and I have a long-term business deal that's been developing over the last few months and I gotta move on it."

They slung their packs and headed through the bar down the stairs. In the stairwell Lopez stopped short and Blooms bumped into him.

"What's wrong, Oscar?"

"Hey, I just remembered somethin'. Boy-san there owes me some bucks. Wait a minute, I'll be right back."

He chased up the stairs leaving Blooms standing there, picking out the patterns in the mosaic tiles of the walls.

Lopez trotted into the bar. "Oh boy-san, you little buddy, where the hell's my change?"

"Ah! There you are. I look for you. Why you go?"

That seems to be a peyote bird design there, Blooms thought, tracing his finger along the tile. I wonder if it really is. I didn't think they had peyote birds over here. The design changed. Lopez and his money and his deals. Well, I hope he strikes it rich, if it don't kill 'em. Ah, for sure this is a scorpion. Lots of those over here, check my boots every time I put them on. Smells like the low end of a rice paddy in here all of a sudden. Wonder why.

"Out of my way, gook. Oh, well if it ain't an Indian."

Blooms turned and saw a man dressed in mixed-up campaign togs. The man stared back through glazed and jaundiced eyes. His sallow skin, marked with open sores, hung from his face. As he walked past Blooms his jowls bounced and he wheezed and coughed. Son-of-a-bitch, Blooms thought. I wonder who the hell he's with. No rank, no unit, no name. I suppose he's headed for the bar. I wonder what Lopez will do when he sees 'em. I better check it out.

Lopez counted the change given to him by the bar boy. As he stuffed the bills into his pocket, he smelled something. He studied the door, waiting.

Months of body waste and blood and guns and spent powder and grease and the pall of rotting bodies preceded the man into the bar. The prostitutes grew still and huddled at their end of the bar, peeking with downturned eyes at the man. He ignored everyone as he sat on the middle stool of the bar.

Lopez checked his uniform to see what type of unit he was from. It struck him that the uniform was odd beyond the fact that he had no patches or rank. Then he realized the uniform consisted of a mixture of North Vietnamese artillery, United States Special Forces, and Chinese mercenary units. The man ordered a beer, and the boy-san ran around in nervous circles trying to get the beer up to the bar. The man reached into his shirt cargo pocked and pulled out something hidden in his fist. He flexed his hand, palm up, to display a human ear, resting dully in place, in his palm. The boy-san whimpered and jumped back. The prostitutes, who had gained a little nerve and moved in to get a better look at this curious product of a war zone, saw what lay in his hand and screamed. The man laughed and drank his beer.

"This ear could get my fifty bucks in Laos or Cambodia." He leaned toward the boy-san. "So how 'bout it, boy-san, good enough for a beer?" He took a bite out of the ear, then set it on the bar.

The boy-san froze, unable to respond, and the man continued drinking, grunting occasionally between swallows. The he set down the beer and faced Lopez.

"What you lookin' at, stud?"

Lopez, inexperienced at the rage he felt, shook where he stood. He had heard stories about irregulars and their units, usually no larger than platoons or companies, that lived in the bush and ambushed or pulled guard for cash or goods. But he never thought he would come in contact with any one of them and he had never tried to confront the rage he always felt when he thought about them.

The man took Lopez's shaking as fear. "You better get out of here, bunny, before I scare you to death. I gotta lot of beer to drink," he laughed.

Lopez was about to reach for a beer and go at the man. Then he remembered the pistol. He reached under his cargo jacket and unstrapped the holster. The man heard it and was about to get up when Lopez drew the pistol and leveled it at his heart. He didn't say anything. He couldn't think of anything to say.

The man laughed at him. "Put the gun down, bunny, or I'll whip you with it."

As he talked, Blooms moved quietly into the bar, edging in close. He picked up an unopened bottle of Bhami-Bha.

The man stood up. As he came up, Blooms swing the bottle down, base first, on the man's head. It made a dull clunking sound, but remained intact, as the man fell back on his stool. The stool swiveled, then deposited him onto the floor in front of Lopez. Blooms put the bottle back on the bar and Lopez holstered the pistol. It was quiet. After a moment a prostitute came over to them.

"He dead?"

They rolled him over and Lopez put an ear down to his mouth.

"He's alive, breathin' at least."

Blooms checked his head.

"Ain't even bleedin' much."

"Why you no kill? He numbah ten thousand GI. He kill beaucoup."

"Listen, honey," Lopez said, "this guy ain't no GI. At least not lately. Besides, I don't have any bullets for this thing." He pointed to the holster.

"Would you shut up, Lopez. This is a hell of a mess. Who is this dude, anyway? I saw him on the stairs."

"I don't know who or what the hell he is. No tags, he ain't no regular. Thanks for bashin' in his head. I was in sort of a jam."

Blooms stared at Lopez. "You're a damn fool, man. Why in hell did you ever pull an unloaded gun on 'em?"

Lopez pointed to the ear still sitting on the bar. "When he pulled that thing out, I just lost it. I just reacted, that's all. I couldn't help it. I . . . I ain't even sorry."

"What's wrong with you, man? I thought you were against killing and all that."

"Maybe I am, but this guy deserves to get his ass killed."

Lopez looked down at the unconscious figure slumped on the floor. He looked out onto the patio, then at Blooms.

"Well, what d'ya suppose we should do with him, Wiley?"

"We?"

"Yeah, you conked him on the head and . . ."

"What you sayin', man? I'm out a' this one. Don't bother me with all this. I'm going' to LBJ, remember?"

"Right!" Lopez scratched his head and paced around the figure. They knelt next to him and went through his pockets. A pile grew, next to him on the floor, containing a cigarette lighter, several M-16 cartridges, a watch, a knife, some MPC, and a little Vietnamese currency. Finally, he pulled out two hand grenade rings connected with a two-foot strand of piano wire. He held up the wire for Blooms to see.

"Know how this works?"

Blooms slipped his middle fingers through the rings and made a short circular motion with his hands and snapped the wire taut. It plunked a dull, fearful note, and the prostitutes, who had crept up to them, stepped back with a whimper.

Finally, Lopez stripped him and piled his uniform and boots in the middle of the patio floor. He went behind the bar and brought back a can of lighter fluid. He soaked the pile and lit it. They watched it burn and the prostitutes and the bar boy stood behind them. Lopez took the knife and Blooms put the grenade rings in his pocket. Both turned to leave, and Lopez noticed the half-eaten ear which was now on the floor next to the man's hand. He pulled out his marijuana pouch and placed the ear in a corner of it, then replaced the pouch. As they entered the street in front of the hotel Blooms spoke to Lopez. They both looked straight ahead.

"That was a funny way to handle that back there, Oscar. What did it prove?"

Lopez cleared his throat. "The prostitutes got his money, boy-san got his watch, and you can count on them calling the QC."

"What can the Vietnamese police do? They take one look at him and you know they'll call the pigs."

"Well, by the time the MPs get there we'll be gone, as least 'til later tonight. I think they'll call in CID 'cause, after not having a uniform, or tags, they're not gonna know anything, except he's probably an American."

"Well, I guess you can think pretty fast, Oscar, for being such a dumb shit. But why d'ya take the ear?"

"Oh, I guess I didn't want to leave it for those people to have to keep lookin' at. They're only civilians, even if they are caught up in the war. Couldn't you see it bothered the hell out of them?"

"Yeah, the women weren't even cryin'."

"I know. That's what bothered me."

"Me too. And it bothers me what that guy's gonna do when he gets his act together. They can't hold him. He'll find something to wear and be out by morning. He knows your face and anybody that takes bounty's probably gonna wanna kill you when he finds you." Blooms looked sidelong at Lopez as they moved through the market.

"We'll be okay if we stick together," Lopez replied.

There was foot traffic on the streets again after the early afternoon heat. Lopez tapped Blooms on the arm. "Okay, Wiley, look for a green door on this side of the market. I smell the fish market so we must be getting close."

They walked slowly now, for it was still hot and they were in a sweat even under the shade awnings. The street people did not favor GIs in their neighborhood. They heard people murmur as they walked by, with an occasional "numbah ten" spoken for them to hear. Several times they were asked to buy heroin, labeled "coke" by the nationals. But they did not buy and they did not show anyone their money and they did not stop along the way.

There were not so many people watching them after that, and when they reached the green door, Lopez turned to Blooms and smiled.

"I suppose you think you know what you're doin'?"

"Don't be cloudy, Wiley. Anyway, if you want to split, I won't stop you."

"You said we should stick together, remember?"

"Sure, but I can't keep you here, and I don't want to turn you in, if that's what you want."

"They'll bust you, Oscar."

"So what? Maybe they'll send me home."

Blooms thought for a moment, then asked. "Where would I go?"

"Saigon. Stay here even. There's a lot of Americans hiding out in the ghetto districts."

"Yeah," Blooms said, "and become another black-market item."

They snickered about that, then grew silent, only standing quietly in front of the green door. It was shut. Lopez peeked through the window and nodded as he recognized the narrow and deep rooms within. There was a wicker chair in the center of the front room, surrounded by several standing mirrors. A bare, incandescent bulb hung down above the chair, swinging slowly in the breeze of a fan set on a table in the corner. He tried the door and it opened. A fly buzzed off into the next room. Blooms followed Lopez, and they moved farther into the room, heading toward a set of plastic-knot curtains that hung in the doorway to the next room.

"What do you want, huh?"

The voice came from behind the curtain. Then they saw a small man in Bermuda shorts and a T-shirt standing in the next room.

They stopped in the middle of the room and Lopez cleared his throat. "Ah, we came to see about a tattoo. Your chair is empty." He pointed at the wicker chair.

"You came to see about a tattoo? And now you see the chair is empty? So what?" He said from behind the curtain.

"Well, I was here once before, with a friend. I thought you might remember me."

"I might. What is your friend's name that you were with?"

"Robert Washington."

"And who are you, and the Indian?"

"I'm Oscar Lopez and this is Wiley Blooms, a friend of mine."

"Yet another friend?"

Lopez shrugged his shoulders and looked around at Blooms, then back at the small man. "Hey look, maybe this is the wrong place, or you're in a bad mood or something. Maybe we should have knocked, I don't know. I came here to do some business, but I feel stupid here so maybe we'll just leave."

"Leave? You've only just arrived. I'm surely in the mood for business. Of course I recognize you, Lopez. I just wanted to see how you were going to act."

He stepped through the curtain and offered his hand to Blooms. "My name is Lloyd."

Blooms took his hand, and the man beamed a toothy, gold-flashing grin. "Now," he said with his ocean blue eyes dressing them up and down, "you want a tattoo. What kind of tattoo would you like then, huh?" He ended the question with a "huh" that sounded like a quarterback barking out signals for a crucial play.

"Kind?"

"Yes, you know. Color, size, design, huh?"

"Oh, oh sure. How 'bout a, a . . ."

"Oh, don't say another word, man. I already know." Then he turned to Blooms. "Tell we, Wiley Blooms, what sort of tattoo are you two after?"

Blooms turned to the little man, then to Lopez. "Search me."

It was quiet for a moment. Lloyd took a long draw on the beer he was holding, wrapped in a terrycloth rag.

Lopez, finally aware that Lloyd was waiting for him to say something, suggested that he try a small blue poppy on the left shoulder blade. The he added, "Just like you give the other GIs that have been here a few times."

"Excellent!" Lloyd exclaimed. "And now tell me, why do you all receive a blue poppy?"

"Because they're all smack freaks, that's why," Lopez answered.

"And you two? How about you two, huh?"

"No, Lloyd," Lopez went on, "I'm a pot head, and Blooms here is a juice freak."

"A pot head and a juice freak, huh?" Lloyd motioned for them to come into the next room. "A pot head, I would imagine, is one who smokes the marijuana. Right?'

They agreed.

"But a juice freak, what's that?" He looked from Blooms to Lopez and back.

"I drink, he smokes," Blooms finally said. "What do you do?"

"Me? Hah! Come sit down, gents, and I'll tell you what I do. The entire street knows you're here, but we needn't advertise the fact." He turned as he spoke, springing from his knees, and wobbling on his bowed legs. "Do let's come in back.

They followed him back through the dim, narrow and windowless frame building.

"There now," he continued after seating them at a small table in the middle of a room farther back from the front. "What do I do? What do I do?" He reflected on the question. "I'm not sure what you mean, Mr. Blooms."

"Nuthin', I don't mean nuthin'"

"I say, is he angry?" Lloyd asked Lopez.

"Nah, but what's so important about what drugs we use."

"Oh, I see, I see," Lloyd replied. "It's really quite simple. You came here to do business and judging from your youth and your lack of rank, I assume you're in the drug market. So you see, by discovering your habits, I've discovered what you're looking for. And all that without asking. Am I right? Huh?'

"What am I looking for then, Lloyd?" asked Lopez.

"Why, since you can get drinks anywhere, it would have to be marijuana."

"Not bad figuring."

"Indeed," Lloyd resumed, "and we'll get to that in due time. But let's just talk for a bit. Care for a beer, huh?"

Neither cared for a beer.

"Very well then, and I hope you don't mind if we do chat for a while. Consider it as part of the cost. You see, I rarely get a chance to converse in English. I do miss the sound of the mother tongue, even though the mother has no use for this prodigal child."

Lloyd spoke rapidly now, and with a certain sort of abandon, while he sat, perched sparrow hawk fashion, on a stool next to the table. He drank again from his beer and looked past them into the front room.

"Tell me though, why do Americans bitch the language so? You all sound like Texans cast in a Shakespearean tragedy or some such other ridiculous juxtaposition."

Blooms tugged at Lopez's sleeve.

"What's he talkin' 'bout, Oscar?"

"Oh, I don't know. I think he's just talking to hear himself talk."

"Oh, I heard that gents, I did. I suspect you're quite right." He sighed, and his face took on a faraway look, then it narrowed, reminding Lopez and Blooms of the room in which they sat.

"Tell me," Lloyd continued, "have you seen Washington lately, huh?"

Lopez coughed. "Well," a long pause followed, "I don't know anyone who's seen him. Have you seen him?"

"Funny you should ask me, wouldn't you think?"

"Lloyd, there's considerable money involved between Washington and me. You know that, too. Want to talk about it?"

"We'll see. We'll see. How much marijuana do you plan to buy?"

"Ten kilos."

"When?"

"Now?"

"Huh?"

"Well, when can I get it?"

"Don't rightly know." Lloyd leaned back on his stool and spoke into the room behind him. A young Vietnamese woman entered the room. They spoke Vietnamese for half a minute, and she left. Then Lloyd turned back to Blooms and Lopez.

"I can get that amount for this figure." He wrote down a number on a paper and pushed it in front of Lopez.

He looked at the figure for a moment with a slight, but not impolite frown. He looked up. "Are we dealing with past debts then, with this?"

Lloyd nodded.

Lopez took the pencil and wrote down his own figure on the paper and pushed it over to Lloyd.

Blooms watched the paper go between them and coughed nervously, which was the only sound that accompanied the ritualistic style of trade.

Lloyd leaned in toward the table and looked at the figure under his own. He had no reaction, except to speak in Vietnamese again. Shortly the girl-san reappeared to listen to his instruction-like tones as she stood behind him. He quit and she left. Then he addressed Lopez and Blooms again.

"Very well then, I think we can do business. I have one more figure to write down, but it will have to wait a bit." He set down his beer and hooked his thumbs through his belt loops. He exhaled deeply and his eyes drifted away. As from a distance he spoke, "I'll have it brought here. You'll only need to wait a little longer, if there's an agreement."

His eyes came back, and he gave quick glances to both of them.

"Are you nervous or something, Lloyd?"

Lloyd leaned into the table, took his thumbs out from his belt loops to rest his elbows on the table in front of him. He took a long and relaxing breath.

"No, I'm not nervous, but I feel a bit weary in the face of misfortune, I guess."

"What do you mean misfortune!" Lopez asked.

"Come on, Lopez, you've been in this neighborhood before. Tell me, what's it like down here? What do you know of this place?"

"Well, I sure as hell wouldn't want to live here, if that's what you mean. But what do you mean?" Lopez sat up to the table.

"Well, to get straight to the point, it was a very stupid thing to have gotten involved with the fellow at the Nha Trang Hotel."

"What fellow?"

"Don't be coy, Lopez. I knew what happened five minutes after it took place. Living here, and dealing in what you call the black-market, one develops an ear for the dialogue on the street. Tell me, Lopez, what do you suppose goes on down here besides the dealing of marijuana?"

Lopez observed that Lloyd was no longer smiling.

"Well, I wonder when the last time was that you gave a tattoo. I've never seen a customer in any parlor, so I guess you must be some sort of dealer in just about anything. I can guess at some of the things, and some of the things I'm better off not knowing. I would even guess that you're a rich man, Lloyd. God only knows why you want to live down here, maybe because the opium's cheaper."

Lloyd relaxed somewhat. "As you Yanks say, 'there it is!' But a man has to make a living, and even living in the black-market, as it were, one can't charge more than the market will bear. You see, the idea is not to make waves, and only go for fifty-one percent of anything, not all of it. I'm giving you this absolutely rock-bottom price on your marijuana because, in a certain way, I'm holding some of your money, via Washington. But mark my words, it's simply a case of self-interest that motivates me to do so. A little profit can keep one fed and alive. Avarice will simply get one killed, in the long run." He finished his beer and set it on the table without a sound.

Lloyd drifted off in his own thoughts. Lopez squirmed on his stool. Blooms looked around the room, wondering how the events in his life had resulted in his being here in some back alley black-market slum.

Finally, Lloyd broke the silence.

"I just don't deal with wastrels I'll have you know. I do have a certain sort of pride in some of what I do. I don't get much of a chance to display what I really care for, at least not to those from the western world. So forgive me if I prattle on, and if I give you a little tour of my back rooms. Twa won't be back for a few minutes yet so I want to show you why I really stay here, and what I really do. I rarely get a chance to shine, you know."

He got up and walked to another plastic-knot door that led to another room. "This way please, gents."

There was a sweet, thick smell in the room they entered. It was shadowy in the room, and they heard breathing and bubbling noises, as they stood where Lloyd had stopped them. Softly a hand guided Lopez's hand to the mouthpiece of a hookah. He inhaled and heard the bubbling noise again and then the sweet smell became a taste and a fog rolled through his brain, rolled up against the back of his skull, along the top and down again through his nose as he exhaled.

"As your eyes can probably see in this dim light," Lloyd went on, "what we have here is a small collection of the old and the invalid of the Nha Trang area. There are many such collections. In the last twenty years or so I have begun the operation of several such establishments."

Blooms and Lopez looked around them. Lopez handed the hookah tip to Blooms who looked at it, then gave it to the girl-san who attended the opium smokers. The smokers reclined in three-tiered bunks along three of the four walls. Along a fourth several invalids squatted or sat on a raised platform and shared a small hookah among themselves. The main hookah rested on a pedestal in the center of the room with several long and flexible stems that reached to the bunks. The girl-san moved through the room passing the mouthpieces from bunk to bunk and refilling the chalice that now glowed and oozed with the black, tarry opium.

Again, there was a long silence while they watched the smoke go round and round. The opium smokers did not notice or did not care that they were being observed. They would bend their heads toward the opium, inhale, and melt back into their bunks and drift through a narcotic trance, hardly breathing.

"These are the people who would die in the streets if someone didn't attend to them. They live and have lived mean lives as witnessed by the fact that the only one they have to take care of them is the likes of me, and a handful of orphan girls I employ."

The girl-san handed the opium to Lopez again. He inhaled deeply, and felt a warm, welcome weight infiltrate his frame. He felt like crawling into one of the empty bunks along the wall. She took it away and offered it to Blooms, who again refused.

"You see," Lloyd continued, "what we have here is somewhat of an Oriental style of social security. The people who live down here, in the fish market, allow me to share in the market. I, in return, collect as many of these people as I can, to keep them off the streets, and give a few young girls a chance to support themselves without having to bed every GI who wants them for five bucks MPC every time they want to eat, or feed a younger brother, sister, or what have you."

The three of them stood in the room. Blooms and Lopez waited for something to happen. Lloyd, long used to observing the behavior of his keep, knew nothing would ever happen to these dead-ended peopled, and was content to observe the two GIs observing the opium smokers.

The girl-san Lloyd had talked to earlier entered through the back of the room and moved over to Lloyd. She spoke softly in Vietnamese to him, and then went back out.

"Come, boys," Lloyd began, "it's time to do business. Let's go back into the other room." He turned them back and followed them through the door and joined them as they sat on the same stools as before. Then he cleared his throat.

"There's some nastiness to be spoken of now, huh?"

"Hmmm?" Lopez asked in a wavering voice.

"Some nastiness, my my, huh?"

"I suppose you're changing your price on me now?"

"Indeed not, Lopez. I wish it was something as meaningless as a little money. But I'm afraid it's a bit more serious, or at least more complicated."

"What's he talkin' about, Oscar?" Blooms asked.

Lopez looked at Blooms and then over at Lloyd, who appeared quite serious and concerned.

"Nastiness?" Lopez asked.

Lloyd straightened up. "Well yes. I'm afraid you mucked things up quite a bit when you pulled that handgun out of your cargo pocket. I really don't know your thinking on that subject, and I don't care to get involved. But let me say this, that fellow's looking for you. He's after your ass."

Lopez shrugged his shoulders. "So what? We're gone tomorrow, probably never be back."

"Yes, but there's tonight. And by now he knows who you are, where you're staying, and what you're up to."

"Oh? How's he know all that?"

"He knows almost as much of what goes on around here as I do. He deals in the black-market, that's how I happen to know him. He used to be in the service, now he's a part-time mercenary."

"That's sort of what I figured him for. How 'bout you, Wiley?"

Blooms shrugged his shoulders. "I'm trying to forget the whole damn thing. I'm the one who put his lights out. I don't know what the hell to think about that."

"He didn't see your face though, huh?"

Lopez stood up slowly and weaved around the table muttering something about opium.

"What's that?" Lloyd asked.

"Nuthin', just nuthin'. Anyway Lloyd, all you said is nasty, I guess, but I guess I don't see anything to worry about."

Lloyd stood up stiffly with his knees cracking. "There's a canvas sack in the back room with ten kilograms of marijuana. It's yours for the second price I wrote out for you."

Lopez looked down at the table where the figures still lie.

Lloyd continued. "Plus another ten dollars. Does that suit you?"

Lopez agreed.

"Now, Lopez, here is something ironic. Where do you suppose I acquired that marijuana, huh?"

Lopez responded to the question by trying to reason out a logical answer, but the opium had taken effect and his brain felt like a slushy tide rolling around in his head.

Lloyd waited a polite moment, then answered his own question. "In terms of ironic situations, it seems quite obvious about the marijuana. But I can see that you are under the effects of the opium. The marijuana, of course, came from the fellow you conked on the bean, huh?"

There was a long silence, then Lloyd continued, "In any event, you must get going. There's an early curfew tonight because of the rocket attacks, and so you're late already. Both my helpers here, Twa and Chien, live in the Nha Trang, sharing a room. They'll take you back there with them now and you can pick up your merchandise in the morning." He turned to the girls and spoke to them in Vietnamese. They nodded their heads and collected their small belongings and acted ready to go. Lloyd turned back to Blooms and Lopez.

"Do you want these two tonight?"

Blooms and Lopez failed to react to such a blunt question, so Lloyd continued. "If you do, I want you to know that any money you give them goes right into their own purses. But I do not want you to think they are prostitutes, or that I'm a pimp."

Blooms and Lopez exchanged glances.

"It's like this, gents, people are forced to do things, in a war zone, that they would not normally do. Take yourselves for instance. Would you do the things back in the United States that you do here? Certainly not. But, if I'm any judge of character, and I believe that I am, you both seem to be fairly good chaps. And that's why I'm saying this to you. Treat these ladies with respect. They are not prostitutes. They are your lovers for one night if you want them. And I judge, by the way you are both standing, that you want them. Now follow them through the alley and stay close."

Twa stood at the door that led to the alley. In the back room the opium dreamers slept or dreamed that people were passing through the room. Chien opened the back door and peeked out. "You come now," she said. Neither Blooms or Lopez heard, so she tapped Lopez on the arm. "We go."

The alley was narrow, and it ran between buildings that faced the street. They were closed in on the sides, so they moved through an open-faced tunnel. Debris and garbage cluttered their path, and they moved cautiously through it so as not to make noise. When they reached intersections, they stopped to check for patrols, then crossed quickly to the next alley. Finally, Twa signaled to them that the next crossing was their last. She motioned for them to step up inside the rear entry of a building while she went to see about the street. She looked back for them and Chien to follow and they all moved at a fast pace until they stopped in front of a red door. Chien listened with her ear to the door, then knocked lightly and waited.

"Chien?' a voice answered softly from behind the door.

Chien answered in Vietnamese. The door opened and they saw an old mama-san standing in the dim light of the closed-down kitchen. This was the Nha Trang Hotel kitchen, and Blooms recognized the old mama-san as the one who had rented him room three seventeen earlier in the day. Twa and the mama-san talked quietly for a while and then the mama-san left. Twa turned to speak with Lopez.

"You come with me. We go upstairs. Mama-san, she beaucoup scared."

"Why?' he asked.

"She say numbah ten you smoke opium. No good, young man no good smoke opium. Opium make you beaucoup deeky-dow."

"How does she know I been smoking opium, Twa?"

"Mama-san, she know everything. She say you stay upstairs." She looked at Lopez. "You sleep with me?"

"Yeah, I'd like that."

"Okay man. We stay three seventeen. Chien stay with your friend in our room. Get up beaucoup early, you go away."

"Okay, but I want to talk to my partner here for a minute. You wait, okay?"

She nodded.

Lopez walked over to Blooms and Chien, who were talking softly in front of the door leading to a small room with two beds in it.

"Hey, Wiley, looks like I'm staying upstairs and you're down here. How's that with you?"

Blooms shrugged his shoulders. "Sounds okay. Chein here's been telling me that mama-san's freaked out 'bout the opium or something. Knows you been smokin' it and can't handle it. I wonder why."

"Oh, who the hell knows. Anyway, we gotta get up real early and I'm really wasted so I'm heading upstairs now. You stickin' around?"

Blooms smiled. "Like I said, Oscar, where would I go?"

"I don't know, maybe look up Lloyd and see what he has to offer or something. Anyway, see ya in the morning."

"Yeah, see ya. Oh yeah, here's the key."

"Thanks, goodnight."

It was cold in the room and Twa moved over to the window and drew it shut. She looked down onto the street. A patrol jeep drove slowly past the front of the hotel. It moved on and then she could hear small arms fire and a few explosions somewhere on the outskirts of Nha Trang.

Lopez relaxed on the bed, his boots still on, watching her as she stood at the window. "Does that scare you, Twa? The firefight?"

She turned to him. "I no scared for me. But my brother, he fight there tonight, maybe."

"Oh? Is he an ARVN?"

"I have one brother who was ARVN. But he die two year ago. Younger brother, he VC. Maybe tonight he fight there." She looked out the window again.

"Come here, Twa, lie down with me. Let's talk." She walked over to the bed and lay down next to him. He breathed deeply and sighed. "You know, girl-san, if I were Vietnamese, maybe I'd be with the VC." He pushed back the hair that was in her face. "You know?"

She nodded.

"Did you bring any opium, Twa?"

She frowned at him but indicated that she had some.

"Fix me a pipe, will you?"

"You smoke, you no wake up in morning."

"No sweat, girl-san, I wake up."

Twa produced a folded piece of aluminum foil that she spread out and placed carefully in the bed. Then she pulled out a short, bamboo pipe from her purse. Lopez watched with diminished curiosity as she kneaded the tarry black opium that was on the foil. She made a tiny ball out of it and jammed it into the pipe. He sat up to take the mouthpiece when she offered it to him. He inhaled as deeply as he could, causing the opium to bubble in the flame she held it to. Again, he felt a fog roll through his brain, coming out his nose as smoke, and also down his spine. His body relaxed. It assumed the contours of the bed and he felt a pleasant and warm weight descend upon the length of his body.

He leaned back, staring at the ceiling, and waited for the overall effect of the opium. The firefight on the outskirts of Nha Trang was over and there was a certain, final silence that seemed to have come with the smoking of the opium. He felt driven along by a free form power that was indifferent to the petty perceptions of a man. Twa looked down at him and saw that soon he would be sleeping. She held his hand and he gave it a slight squeeze, reassuring her that he was still aware of her. She took off his boots and helped him get his uniform off. Then she slipped out of her ao dai, under which she wore nothing, and crawled under the light blanket with Lopez, who was already asleep.

In the room of Chien and Twa, the room next to the hotel kitchen, Blooms sat in an undersized wicker chair next to a Sears and Roebuck floor model lamp, and Chien sat on the bed next to him. The lamp was burning, dimly now, because of the reduced nighttime power, and the single window, which looked out into the alley, was drawn and shuttered. They too noticed that the firefight had ended, but they were not assured that the night would remain peaceful. They both hid this, however, as do men and women who have seen the worst of bad situations and managed to live through them.

"Why you friend have a gun, Blooms?"

Blooms tried to rearrange himself in the chair and she patted the bed next to her. As he moved over next to her he spoke.

"He's s'posed to be guarding me."

"Him guard you? He beaucoup deeky-dow. Smoke beaucoup opium." She looked at him as if she had uncovered a well-hidden fact of his life. "Why he guard you, man?"

Blooms scratched his head and squirmed around next to her and tried to look through the uncooperative window.

"No sweat man. You no say why, no sweat." She rummaged around in her purse. "You smoke cunsai?" She held up a bag of marijuana for him to inspect.

He held it to the light, fingered it and smelled it.

"Where'd you get this, girl-san. It looks like a bunch we had back in Dalat last month, from Laos."

"Twa has brother. He bring, sell to GI."

"Oh? This GI, you know him?"

Chien gave him an insulted stare.

"Was his name Washington?"

She smiled at the sound of the name. "You know Washington? He numbah one GI. How you know Washington?"

"Same unit, up in Dalat. Or at least we were. No one's seen him in a while." Blooms remembered what Lopez said about the desertion of Washington. "Have you seen him, girl-san?"

She gave him another insulted look and he knew that she had.

"It's okay, Chien. He's my friend. I'd like to know if he's okay and everything. Have you?"

She looked away from Blooms, down at the bag of marijuana.

"He okay. I see him two day ago."

"Two days! Where'd you see 'em, girl-san?"

"Nha Trang. He work for Lloyd, go Saigon, Pleiku, Nha Trang, beaucoup city."

"When's he comin back?"

She shrugged her shoulders, and it went quiet in the room. She took a pipe from the tabletop text to the bed and stuffed it with a big pinch of marijuana. Then she gave the pipe to Blooms, who waited as she lit it for him. They shared the pipe in silence, passing it back and forth. Blooms took off his boots and sat his pack against the headboard, stretching his legs over the foot of the bed. She emptied the ashes in the pipe and joined him.

Blooms leaned over and ran his hand up and down her flat stomach.

"I have a girlfriend like you at home."

"She Vietnamese?"

"No, Crow."

"What you mean, Crow?"

"She's an Indian, like me."

She nodded. "You not same-same Lopez, beaucoup other GI. That make you numbah ten, huh?"

Blooms grunted an approval. "There it is, girl-san, there it is."

"Washington, he say same thing. He say you no have white skin, you numbah ten in United States."

"Yeah, that's about it, I guess." He began unbuttoning her shirt and was having difficulty, so she helped.

"I no believe that. You live United States, why you say that numbah ten, man?"

Blooms smiled and shook his head.

"Same-same here."

She started unbuttoning his cargo jacket. "Someday, maybe I go United States. No war there. War here kill everyone someday, maybe." She reached up and turned off the light and slipped off her silk pants.

"Washington, he say he stay in Vietnam long time, maybe forever. He say war over soon. Vietnam better place for him than United States."

"I don't know, Chien. I see plenty of Vietnamese who hate black GIs and Indian GIs but love white GIs. Why's that?"

"I say before, Vietnam same-same United States. But nobody fight in United States. No war. Not same-same." She helped him get out of his cargo pants and then they lay in the dark, under her poncho liner, and learned the feel of each other's skin.

"Washington, he say he live in . . . city of brother love. You know that?"

"Yeah, I think that's Philadelphia."

"Yeah, Phiradelphia. Only he say if you have black skin, not same-same for all. You bek?"

Blooms grunted.

"Washington, he say he like Vietnam, no like United States. Same-same you? You no like United States?"

Blooms sat up in bed. "You ask a lot of questions, you know that?"

"You no like?"

"Well, it's just that I can't answer those questions for me, so how can I answer 'em for you? Dig it?"

Chien lightly moved on top of him and kissed him with smiling lips. "All GI same-same. They no bek nothing."

In Nha Trang, the birds still sang in the morning, and Twa heard them in the moment of pre-dawn light. She opened her eyes and saw Lopez sleeping quietly and evenly next to her. Both she and Chien were due at Lloyd's by sunup to feed and tend the dreamers that Lloyd had watched over during the night. She rose in silent movement, dressing quickly, made a toilet, and headed for the kitchen. She met Chien there, and together they prepared tea for themselves, making petit, tinkling noises that punctuated the stillness of the still, early dawn. They finished their cups, washed them, and went out the alley door. The old mama-san, who had let them in the night before, stirred in her bed behind the stove, rose, and locked the door behind Twa and Chien.

Blooms was dreaming but he did not know it. In his dream he kept saying he wished it was only a dream. But it was too real, he thought, to be anything but waking reality. Wild painted war ponies ran over the land, and he knew the land. It was the Wichita Mountains, not far from his home, the source of his blood. And he was small, the ponies rushed past him, their crazed eyes flashing down at him. He was not afraid for they saw him and flew past in deft lunges, over and around. He saw the mountain, far away, and it compelled him to search for something, to move. And he knew that by moving and searching, it was he who would be found. The ponies grouped on the far ridge, turned, and watched him as he headed for the mountain. He felt that he walked on his knees, and if he tried to run, the earth, even though bone dry and crusted into clumps of clay and sand, sucked at his bare feet, and pulled him down. So he walked and looked, and listened.

Then he heard the flute, and he knew that Roland had found him. He smiled, and his laugh which followed was the laugh of a child who has been looking for a surprise and has just found it. He poured out a long and uncontrollable giggle and the giggle made him laugh some more. It flowed off his tongue and Roland mimicked it on his reed flute. He trilled the notes and over-blew into the octaves unheard by men and he was answered by the throaty screech of the peyote bird who darted past Blooms and headed for the sun. Roland came out of the sun, tall and slowly bobbing, his long black hair waving in response to his walk. His eyes glowed with the power from another world, but they smiled at Blooms with compassion, wisdom, and joy. Blooms ran to him, the earth releasing him, and he laughed again in reply to Roland's flute. Roland faced the mountain, to the north, and they began their journey. They walked and walked and Blooms was thirsty and hot and dry. Roland reached in his pocket and pulled out a button-like cactus. He gave it to Blooms. Blooms looked at it and it was green and gray and soft, fresh and supple. He ate it. They walked and walked. They walked for a year. There was snow but it was not cold. There was high sun but it was not hot. There was night but there was not fear. There was day but there was not drudgery.

All there was, was Roland's flute, and space.

They walked and walked, and after a year they stood at the foot of the mountain. Roland put away his flute and they climbed. By evening they pulled themselves onto the plateau that was the top of the mountain. They breathed deeply in the rarefied air, and they watched the sun, covering half the west, pulling the gown of night behind it. Blooms closed his eyes, and he heard the pastel colors of twilight pouring lightly into his ears, to glow inside him.

Roland blew soft notes on his flute and Blooms smelled the notes as they came to him and turned in his stomach. This made him sick, but in his head, and in his dream, which he did not perceive as a dream, he saw Roland press softly on his stomach, and the sickness left him.

He opened his eyes. Roland pointed to a rock design spread out at their feet. The small stones, arranged in concentric circles, with spurs pointing in the primary directions, stood for the important people in Bloom's life. He saw the stone that was Roland, and then grandmother, great-uncle, his sisters, parents, they were all there. But in the middle, he saw a C-ration can, open and empty. He bent over the circle to see inside the can. A small scorpion lay inside at rest at the bottom of the can.

Blooms raised his eyes and found Roland, who began fingering his flute. He did not blow, but Blooms knew he was fingering the notes that belonged to the favorite tune of Lopez's girlfriend.

And the words to that tune came to him in Vietnamese and he knew what they meant. They told him this was a dream, and that he would never remember the dream until he stood on top of the mountain and placed his own stone in the center of his circle.

Lopez opened a can of C-rations and immediately smelled the contents. His stomach turned over and he knew it was another dose of the Army's ham and eggs. But it was not ham and eggs. Instead, there was a scorpion. He tried to move away but could not. The scorpion crawled over his hand and up his arm and under his cargo jacket. It came out from under his shirt and moved over his collarbone. It rested on his throat, and he knew it would sting him, but he could not move. The scorpion snapped its tail and there was pain that raced to his heart. Then the scorpion vanished, and the pain centered in his left ear: he knew he would wake up now, for during all of this time he felt the presence of something at the door, and that something was about to come through the door. He wanted to be awake and to respond, but something told him to be still, to sleep. Except that now the door was open, and he knew he should be awake. The something turned into a man standing over him who was stringing a wire through his fingers. He smelled jungle rot. He really should wake up now. But he could not, and he knew he was dead.

Blooms heard the pots and pans banging in the kitchen and he sat up. He looked out the window and he could see that it was an hour or so after sunrise. Guess I overslept. I wonder if Oscar remembers where I am. He rolled out of the small bed and dressed.

The kitchen was busy, and no one bothered with him. The old mama-san, who was washing vegetables, watched him and shook her head as he walked through the kitchen and into the hallway that led to the stairs. He wondered, as he walked slowly up the stairs, if they would reach LBJ today. It was already too late for getting an early flight to Ton Son Nhut. Maybe it would take another day. Oh well, he thought, I'm not in charge here.

He reached the third floor and walked down the hall to three seventeen. He stood outside the door and listened for any sounds from the room. All was quiet.

"Oscar?"

Again, all was quiet, and he tried the door. It was open.

"Oscar? I'm comin' in. It's late and we gotta get on the road."

Then he smelled the jungle rot, and he knew he should get in the room right away. He saw Lopez's boots placed on the floor next to the bed and then he saw the blood and the body at rest on the bed. The sheet was soaked with blood, and he knew that the body under the sheets was dead.

"God!"

Blooms walked over to the bed and pulled back the sheet. Lopez's body was permanently at rest, on top of the bed, soaked in its own blood that had thickened and was already bringing flies. He stared at the body, with its head tilted back, exposing a thin slit that ran across the throat, the head fell over to the side. The left ear was missing.

"God damn!"

Blooms stared down at the body for a moment, then walked over to the door and locked it. He looked around the room and found Lopez's handgun and holster piled on the nightstand, along with his billfold. He strapped the holster on beneath his cargo jacket and stuffed the billfold into his pack. The travel orders were sticking out of Lopez's backpack, and he took them, too. As he took them out of the pack he saw the marijuana pouch, and he grabbed that as well. He ripped the name tag from Lopez's cargo jacket and began looking for his tags, then remembered that he never carried them.

He looked at the body and went in the bathroom and started to throw up. Nothing came, so he dropped his pants and sat on the stool.

"They're gonna think I done it," he said under his breath. "Sure as hell, they're gonna think I done it. I gotta get the hell out a' here."

He strapped on his pants and walked into the room, not looking at the body except to flip the sheet up over the head, and walked out into the hall. He locked the door and hung the "do not disturb" sign on the knob. The hall was empty, so he ran to the stairs. There was a maid on the stairs, so he walked past her in a normal pace, and then threw himself down the rest of the flights. When he reached the main floor, he saw the path was clear to the front entrance.

The street was filled with market goers. He mixed with them, while trying to picture the face of the ex-GI at the bar. But the face would not appear. He felt like throwing up again, and realized it was the smell of the fish market that was making him sick. His pack dug into his shoulders and he decided to sit on the curb for a minute. Maybe I should get drunk, he thought.

"Blooms? What in heaven's name are you doing. I should think you and Lopez would have picked up your merchandise by now and be halfway to Saigon. Are you well? Huh?"

Blooms recognized Lloyd's voice but didn't look up.

"Very well, never mind that now. You won't do very well for yourself perched like an orphan on this curb. Say what? Have you flown the coop, so to speak?" Lloyd glistened in the morning sun. He beamed down on Blooms, who squinted back up at him from the curb.

Just what I need, Blooms thought. He looked down at the curb and followed the progress of a cockroach that hunted for food between his boots. Lloyd held out his hand to help him up, but Blooms pushed it away and stood up on his own.

"Stroke of luck, wouldn't you think, Blooms, that we should chance to meet this way? I don't ordinarily take my steam bath on even days of the week. That's where I've just come from, don't you see?" He pointed to a steam bath entrance a few yards away. "However, an associate is due momentarily and I shall be quite busy for the next day, huh?"

Blooms, who had been watching the street in the direction of the hotel, turned to Lloyd.

"Why don't you just get the hell on your way or I'll heave on your nice canvas shoes."

Lloyd coughed. "Very well then. I just thought you might be interested in knowing who my associate is. In any event, see you later."

"What do you mean by that? I'm not exactly stationed here." Blooms sighed. "Shit. I gotta get goin'." He moved away.

"Blooms" Why do you force such bluntness from me? Just where the hell would you be going, huh?"

Blooms stopped and turned around. "I . . . I don't know."

"Back to the hotel? Three seventeen perhaps?" Lloyd asked.

"No. "I'm goin' to the . . ."

"The air terminal? And show your special orders?"

Blooms watched Lloyd's eyes to see if they might tell what he was really getting at. But Lloyd put forth an idle sort of answering stare.

In the silence between the two men standing in the market traffic, decisions that had to be made soon began shaping into words.

"You know Lopez's been killed?" Blooms asked.

Lloyd blinked. "Yes, yes, I do. Seems a pity."

"Everyone's gonna think I done it. I didn't do it. I just came in his room and there he was. A real mess. People's gonna think I done it. I didn't do it though." Blooms dropped a tear that soaked into the red dust on the boulevard. "I just came in the . . ."

"Yes, I know Blooms. Or I should say I at least I don't doubt your word."

"I . . . I don't know what to do. I can't go nowhere, and I can't stay here and Lopez, he was crazy, crazy as hell for lettin' himself get killed like that, but he didn't give me no shit and now I don't . . ."

"Huh? Back up man. You're not the only one in a jam you know. How do you think it looks to have a dead GI in your favorite hotel, huh? And what's to be done with the corpse?"

Blooms rubbed his eyes. "Yeah, I guess, but I still don't know what to do about . . ."

"Well, I'll tell you, if you're willing to listen now. Huh?"

Blooms nodded.

"Very well then but do let's get off the street. Come along with me to the ice factory down by the docks. It's cool there and I have a bit of an office there. Best for you not to be seen, huh?"

Blooms agreed to follow Lloyd through the narrowing streets while the stench of the fish market grew stronger. But he no longer felt nauseous, now that the future had balanced out against the last hour.

They walked in under the tin roof of the ice plant and the change in temperature raised goose flesh on Bloom's skin. The salt in the air made him sneeze. The plant workers turned to look at him and laughed.

"I learned long ago to breath out while passing through here." Lloyd said over the laughter. "These fellows here take pride in their briny lives and tend to see sneezing as a sign of weakness. By the way Blooms, do you have Lopez's billfold and tags and travel orders and the like? Mustn't let them get into the wrong hands."

Lloyd showed Blooms through a door and into a small room with a desk and three chairs and cardboard boxes arranged to serve as filing cabinets. Lloyd sat down behind the desk and put his feet up on the desk. He pulled out a drawer, rummaged around, and came out with a Cuban cigar packed in an aluminum tube. "Ah, the flavor of old Havana!"

He smiled at the cigar as he slid it out of the tube, then stared across the desk at Blooms, who sat himself down.

"Well, Wiley? We must have the papers and such. Do you still have them?"

"What d'ya need 'em for anyway?"

Lloyd nipped the butt end of the cigar and spat it on the floor. He pulled a lighter from his pocket and lit the cigar, making a moist, smacking noise as he drew in the flame. He bent over the desk, pointed his head through the smoke to stare at Blooms.

"Are you naive, or something?"

"Maybe so. But why should you get Lopez's stuff. He had some bucks, you know."

"I don't give a damn about the money, man! Don't you see what I'm dealing with here?"

"Ah, no. No, I don't. I don't see nothin'"

"Okay, okay Blooms, listen. You see, Lopez's untimely death has put our collective ass in a jam, huh? Up until now, this area of Nha Trang has been relatively bloodless. At least no GIs have been killed down here. And the neighborhood has thrived because of this. But if they find out officially about this, this mess, that is, if your government gets the body, or any papers and the like, well, it would be unfortunate for our little family. Don't you see?"

"What the hell does the United States care about another dead GI in 'Nam?"

"Well, I suspect they wouldn't care much if it happened out in the bush or some such thing. More easily explainable. But Nha Trang is an open city. GIs dying within it would tend to close it right down. And then there goes a goodly amount of business."

Lloyd looked past Blooms toward the door. He smiled, nodded his head, and motioned for someone to come in. Blooms turned to see who was there. It was Washington, standing in the doorway, filling the space with a flowing gold and purple, silk tunic, stateside blue jeans, and Viet Cong sandals. He wore a gold ring in his left ear, and a gold star filling in one of his front teeth.

"Washington!"

Blooms sprang from his chair and picked up Washington in a bear hug, setting him down and took his hand in the traditional handshake.

"Man am I glad to see you!"

"I know you are man. I would be too if I was you."

"Yeah, yeah, I guess. What in hell you been doin'? No one knows what happened to you and we . . ."

"Talk 'bout it later Wiley. Plenty of time for that. I been listenin' to you 'n Lloyd here. It sounds like you don't trust 'em. That right?" Blooms turned to face Lloyd. "I don't know what to think 'bout nothin'. You trust him, Washington?" Washington laughed. "Hell no! But then he don't trust me either. Works better that way. But, you see, we got alternatives to trust. And Blooms, right about now, you ain't got no alternatives." Blooms sat down again, and Washington sat down next to him.

Lloyd took a long draw on his cigar. "You see, Wiley, it's absolutely paramount that we have Lopez's things. We suspect that you have them."

Blooms searched Washington's face for an answer. Washington nodded his head. "Okay, I got his orders in my pack." He reached in his pants pocket. "Here's his billfold." He tossed it on the desk. "Just for the hell, I took off his name tag. Here."

"And his dog tags?" Lloyd asked.

"No dog tags. He never carried 'em."

Lloyd looked over to Washington.

"Yeah, that's right," Washington said. "A lotta dudes in the artillery don't carry 'em."

Lloyd cleared his throat. "Very well then. Robert, fetch out those orders please, and we'll get down to business." Washington reached into Blooms' pack and yanked out the packet of travel orders that were sticking out of the flap. He looked them over and then set them on the desk in front of Lloyd.

"Seem to be in order, Lloyd. Now what?"

"Only two things left to do, huh?"

Blooms looked at Washington, then at Lloyd. "What's that?"

"Get rid of them, of course. Make the final erasures of Lopez's existence." Lloyd reached over and picked up the billfold. He took everything out of it, made one pile of money and one pile of papers. He pushed the pile of money toward Blooms. "Here, Wiley, you've had a hard morning, you should probably have this."

Blooms stared at the money in front of him, then shook his head.

"Take it, man," Washington said. "You gotta have it."

Blooms sighed, then collected the money and stuffed it in his jacket pocket.

Lloyd collected the pile of Lopez's papers and the travel orders and placed them in a metal wastepaper basket next to the desk.

"Match?"

Blooms drew a farmer's match from his pocket and handed it to Lloyd.

"Thank you." He struck the match with his thumbnail, and it burst into flame. Then he dropped it in the basket.

Lloyd stood up and walked around the desk to the door. He turned to Blooms.

"You probably are wondering what is going to happen to you. Do you turn yourself in, and then run the risk of spending the rest of your life in the stockade for an offense you didn't commit? Who would believe you? And if you don't turn yourself in, then what do you do?"

Blooms shook his head.

"You work for me. That's what you do. Just like Robert here. I also deal in deserters. They work cheap, it's never an easy thing to desert. Everyone gets the wrong impression. But I don't get the wrong impression, huh?"

He walked over and placed his hand on Bloom's shoulder.

"So, for now, at least, you better stick with us. If things work out, someday, if you want, you could even go back home."

He walked out of the room.

They sat quietly, listening to the workings of the ice plant beyond the office wall. The image of Lopez's body pushed its way through the haze of Blooms's jumbled thoughts. He hung his head, and a tear dropped on his dusty, scarred boot. Roland and Lopez really are alike, he thought. Even more, now, because they're both so dead. And they died the same way, sort of. And I guess I don't really care that Oscar's dead. Just bein' in the 'Nam can make you dead. It's just the way he died. Maybe if he was on patrol or something, but to be dead when you don't expect it. It was the same with Roland. Blooms sighed and shook his head. His shoulders shook involuntarily.

"I know, Blooms, it's a bummer." Washington broke into Blooms's thoughts. "It's a bitch, but Lopez was careless. He weren't careful. He was in the wrong place, at the wrong time. You can't go showin' your heater to a god damned mercenary without somethin' happening. All you done, Wiley, when you used that bottle, was postpone it some. Lopez was as good as dead, when he flashed that .45, unless he pulled down on 'em. And you're lucky you didn't get nailed too. And you gotta play it real cool 'til we can get you the hell out a' here."

Washington stopped, and the little office filled with mournful stillness again, and Blooms saw Lopez again, floating toward him through a series of scenes. The body floated through the long nights on guard, in the towers standing above the circles of concertina and barbed wire. He heard Lopez's voice softly questioning him on what it was like to be an Indian. At first, he thought Lopez was joking, but the tone of his voice told him different. He seemed to care. He was never serious, but he was always sincere.

And he saw Lopez's body floating ahead of him on patrol, when they simply knew they would draw an ambush. Sometimes it was inevitable, but you only knew after it was over, when you were waiting to get picked up. He saw Lopez using his sawed-off twelve-gauge shotgun like sonar. He almost felt out the situation with the muzzle and sometimes, maybe because he was careless, like everyone knew, he threw off the ambush and he would tip everyone off and hardly anyone ever got hit, or at least you tried to forget that part. And when you forget, you forget everything, even though sometimes the explosions knocked you down and the flashing hell-colored red, framed in hell-colored black made you lose control and you would have to change into the extra cargo pants you always took along, just in case. Maybe this is all over for me now, Blooms thought. Maybe I'm out of the war for good. Lopez is.

Lopez would talk on guard to stay awake, and smoke pot, Blooms remembered, because he said if he got real fucked-up, he just couldn't fall asleep. He remembered the morning Lopez called in that there was a huge bamboo horse, on a platform on wheels, standing at the gate of the firebase.

"It's fucking huge," he said, "and I'm gonna haul it inside and the war will be over, and we'll end up in Italy if we're lucky." Nobody knew what he meant, and we all thought he was crazy. But then he explained Troy to me, and it all made sense. Maybe he did see that horse.

And he thought of Lopez at the base camp where he tried to build an airplane out of two-by-fours and plastic sheeting.

"I'm gonna fly myself home," he yelled, "and I'm takin' all my girlfriends home with me, and we're gonna live in the woods, next to a lake, and fish, and have a garden and grow tons of pot."

Then he'd sit down next to the mess he had built and smoke and look at it. Everyone laughed and shook their heads, and walked away sayin' things like, "That Lopez, he's crazy, he's a crazy-ass pot head." But they quit laughin' when they found out he'd stolen the lumber they wanted to use to start a new NCO club after the old one took a 122 rocket through the front door. That's when he started walking point on recovery patrols.

Blooms laughed under his breath. "Lopez was pure, fucked-up crazy." He looked at Washington. "Wasn't he?"

Washington agreed with him as he stood up. He turned to Blooms and motioned for him to follow. They headed out onto the ice plant wharf toward a boat house. He unlocked it and they entered.

"The papa-san who takes care of the wharf here, you know, helps the boats dock and stuff like that, well, he also works for Lloyd."

"Seems everyone works for Lloyd."

"There it is. Anyway, his wife's papa-san, you know, papa-san-in-law? He stays at one of Lloyd's smoke houses."

"Smoke houses?"

"Yeah, you know, an opium den. Anyway, papa-san does little odd jobs for Lloyd in order to pay for the opium and a little rice."

"So what?"

"Well, papa-san also works for the city. He makes sure all the garbage from the fish market gets hauled away or goes out with the tide. Gets his own personal sampan for the job. See?" He pointed down some steps to where a sampan rose and dropped with the swell. "And, "Washington sighed, "today he made an extra pick up."

"At the Nha Trang?" Blooms asked.

"There it is. But papa-san, he don't like haulin' 'round dead GIs, 'specially with their throats slit open. He don't want any more to do with it."

Blooms nodded his head.

"So," Washington hesitated, "so your first job is with me, right here, right now."

"What's that?"

"Helping me dump Lopez."

Blooms watched the sampan gliding up and down. He imagined the face of his grandmother and he knew she was thinking about him. Her puzzled eyes sought him out, seeking an explanation for the confusing and emotional energy she was receiving from her grandson. Her eyes understood something then, and she began keening for an unknown reason for a soul lost in an opium den.

Washington touched his shoulder. "Come on Wiley, let's get it over with. He was my friend too, you know, the crazy son-of-a bitch."

"Yeah, all right, okay. Where the hell is he?"

"He came in on the garbage cart and papa-san put him down in the sampan. We got to put on some a' these gook clothes papa-san left for us, and pour a load of garbage on top a' the sampan, to cover it all up, you follow? Then we we haul it out into the harbor and dump the whole load, right? There it is. Papa-san and me wrapped him up in his sheets and tossed in some rock salt to keep him on the bottom 'til the tide carries 'em out."

It was one o-clock. The sun beat down, flattening Nha Trang harbor and even the sea's undulations seemed defeated by the heat. Most sensible people tried for some sleep. But those who did not, and who happened to see the sampan that edged toward the depth of the harbor, might have guessed that it was time for the garbage to be dumped. The boy-sans in the vessel moved slowly. One was dark skinned. Perhaps he was Cambodian. They stopped somewhere toward the middle, where the tide was strongest, and they dumped their garbage.

But the boy-sans stood looking into the water. Then they lifted another bundle from the bottom of the sampan. They slid it over the side and stood there again, watching the water. One of them took something from a small pouch, something wrapped in a handkerchief. He unwrapped it and took something out. Then he threw it in after the bundle.

"I'm sorry, Lopez."

You fly?
Wiley looks at you
he looks unsure
he laughs, and takes the wheel
he chases a cloud
the wings ripple and the airframe shudders
the major takes back the wheel
you pick up the South China Sea and follow the coastline
to Na Trang
but you land too late to make your flight to Long Binh
you walk on the beach
the white sand goes for miles
you ignore the concertina
you ignore the gun ships
Wiley points to the tiny seashells
he wonders how many there are
you say one trillion
he asks if he can have some
you nod, and he fills his pockets
the next day, at Long Binh Jail, they take his seashells,
and lead him away
you are the one he listens to
you are his only friend
full moon pulls the tide offshore

Yobo Shibo

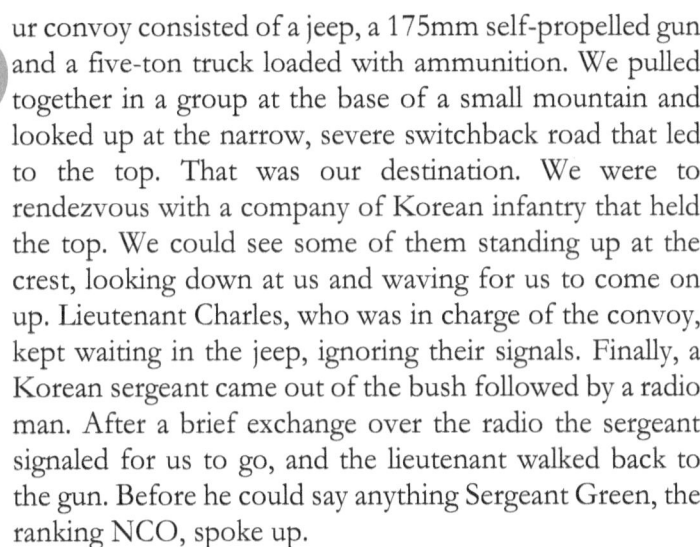ur convoy consisted of a jeep, a 175mm self-propelled gun and a five-ton truck loaded with ammunition. We pulled together in a group at the base of a small mountain and looked up at the narrow, severe switchback road that led to the top. That was our destination. We were to rendezvous with a company of Korean infantry that held the top. We could see some of them standing up at the crest, looking down at us and waving for us to come on up. Lieutenant Charles, who was in charge of the convoy, kept waiting in the jeep, ignoring their signals. Finally, a Korean sergeant came out of the bush followed by a radio man. After a brief exchange over the radio the sergeant signaled for us to go, and the lieutenant walked back to the gun. Before he could say anything Sergeant Green, the ranking NCO, spoke up.

"God almighty, sir. The road's too steep for the track or the five-ton and the switchbacks are too tight. I don't think we can make it up."

"We've got to try, sergeant," Lieutenant Charles explained. "It's almost dark and we're sitting ducks down here. It's either make it or nothing. Let's go."

"Yes, sir. Then we'll make 'er."

Sergeant Green walked back to the gun where Louie, the driver, Big, the gunner, and I waited.

"The Lt. says we gotta go for it so follow the jeep and I'll ride in the five-ton." Louie," he went on, "don't let the outside track slip over the edge. Hug the upper side of the bank all the way and have someone guide you through the switchbacks."

Louie nodded, revved the huge diesel motor that rumbled only a few inches from him and dropped the track into gear with a hard clank. The gun lurched forward, and the overextended barrel dipped down to within a yard of the steeply inclined road ahead. By now the lieutenant's jeep was already waiting at the first of the switchbacks. Big nodded to me and I hopped off the track to help guide it around the turn. I looked up the face of the mountain and counted twelve more switchbacks before the road reached the crest. At this rate, I thought, it would be well after dark before we reached the top, but the closer we come to the bivouac the better we'll all feel. By now the Koreans were sending down two squads to post along the road and the patrol at the base of the mountain came up the rear. The sentries along the steep bank all waved as we rolled by. I looked back down to watch the five-ton, loaded with hundreds of high explosive projectiles with a trailer full of powder, haul itself tiredly up the long runs of the narrow, rut filled road. As it rounded each switchback, the trailer would jut out precariously over the edge of the bank and Sergeant Green, acting like a mother hen, would give frantic signals for his driver, the Bone, to go by. Soon we outdistanced them and finally we lost them in the shadows of the evening and the dust from the road.

As we closed on the crest the last remnants of the evening faded. In the darkness the Koreans guided us into a beehive of foxholes, temporary bunkers and trenches that were barely distinguishable from the large rocks, stumps and mounds of dirt that littered the top. I felt like I was dreaming as I walked ahead of the gun into the camp. The powdery soft dust fluffed around me as if I were floating. Faces of smiling Koreans floated by me, all pointing to where the track was to be secured for the night. They performed small, reassuring gestures with their hands that appeared disengaged from the body while in the blackness a hand would wave, pointing me, and the track, in the right direction. We were all tired and the Koreans knew that we had traversed back-to-back Viet Cong strongholds that day, only to stop here, in the middle of a third stronghold. They were impressed by our pluck but realized that the limited size of our convoy enabled us to move quickly and without fanfare. They were ready to welcome us. We offered them a certain type of security, either real or assumed, that automatically accompanies field artillery.

The Koreans had secured this mountaintop weeks before after days of inching their way up to the top under concentrated mortar attacks, fire fights, booby traps and even, their commander was to tell our lieutenant, small avalanches of rocks and debris. It was the company's first real contact after too many months of itching for a fight and they were proud of their victory, if that's what such a thing can be called. Now they were pulling special operations in the valley and had located numerous bunkers and tunnels that were well defended at times. The Korean commander had convinced himself that the Viet Cong were using the bunkers and tunnels as a base for supply and ambush operations throughout the valley. Our heavy artillery could knock out the bunkers and permit his infantry to conduct a more meaningful operation afterward. Meaningful operations, for the Koreans, meant killing as many of "the enemy" as possible, for their homeland, according to them, was in real danger because of the insurgency in South Vietnam. The Koreans, first and foremost, were Asians and their presence in combat zones always cast a shadow over the entire operation. It stood as more proof that an outside force could turn people of somewhat the same ilk against one another. It also made for ferocious one-upmanship in the field, with both sides, or sometimes three or four sides, if you want to include the NVA or the United States, trying to break the will and the psych of the enemy by committing heinous acts that no one would dare counter.

The commander of the Korean infantry, I think he was a captain, all decked out in his military paraphernalia, from a netted, camouflaged helmet to field puttees, met us as we entered his bivouac. His lieutenants and senior sergeants flocked around him in some sort of ancient oriental subservience, very eager and willing to do his bidding. He directed us to pull up to the highest point on the hilltop and head the gun out toward a long, deep, dark valley that stretched out to the east.

Louis complied and then shut down the powerful motor that drove the gun. He pulled himself out of the driver's pit and sat there on the gun for a moment looking down the barrel and into the valley. "The Valley of the Shadow . . ." he said quietly to himself, and then plodded off in search of something to drink. Big, the gunnery sergeant, slapped me on the back and almost knocked me off the gun. He was standing on the gun himself and laughing at me. We were good friends, and I knew he was fooling around but it still made me mad so I dove at him, driving both of us off the gun and onto the ground. I landed on top of him and he let out a grunt as we both hit. But he only laughed again as he wrapped me in a bear hug. I stand six feet tall and weigh close to two hundred pounds, but I felt frail and helpless in Big's grasp. He just barely got in the service at six feet five inches and weighed two hundred forty pounds at the time. Big, whose real name was Elliot Bush, never really forced his size on anyone, though, and even though he could have crushed the air out of me, he told me he gave up and then let go, suggesting we go find a drink, too. We'd been on the road since dawn and now it was dark again. We were caked with grease and dust. The lines in our faces reminded me of maps which led nowhere but now we were secure for the night, and it was time to unwind. On our way to find Sergeant Green, who had just pulled in with the five-ton truck, we introduced ourselves to a Korean sergeant who had been watching us wrestle. He looked even more gung-ho and resolute than his captain, but he at least could smile, even if it was with a faint portion of sardonic mischief. For a Korean he was huge, standing very close to six feet and topping the scales at maybe one hundred ninety pounds. He stood solidly in his place, packed into his uniform and we could tell he was a human dynamo just by watching his strong, nimble hands, with which he was juggling three tennis balls.

Big smiled, saying hello and offering his hand. The Korean stopped juggling and grasped Big's hand. They didn't shake, but rather only squeezed each other's hand for a moment before they both laughed and let go.

"Hello," Big said again. "I'm Sergeant Bush and this here's Corporal Adams."

I shook hands with the Korean and even though I'm far from being a pansy, my hand felt like a flower in his grip. But he smiled kindly and released.

"Yobo shibo," he said enthusiastically. Then he started beguiling us with some rather astute juggling tricks.

Big and I scratched our heads, looked at each other, shrugged our shoulders and plodded off to find something to drink. We found Sergeant Green, who had already set up a water station and was engaged in casual conversation with Lieutenant Charles about what seemed to be a pretty good set up. There were about a hundred Koreans on the hilltop, all inspired, either through their own will or through the will of their commander, into a crack outfit that was completely alerted and begging for more action. They had obviously been given a pep talk and informed to treat us cordially and not to interfere with "the strange habits of the Americans."

The four of us, who represented the ranking members of the gun section, relaxed around the small potable water blivet as other members of the section came by for water and a ration of beer. The Bone, who had just parked the five-ton, caught my attention and drew me off behind a small bunker.

"Hey, Blackie! Man, did we score some righteous dew in that last village where we broke down. You should try it. Everyone else is just blasted."

"How much did you get?"

"We bought a kilo for a case of C's and twenty bucks, MPC," The Bone answered. "I hopped off the five-ton and found a boy-san to help me look for some while you guys fixed the jeep."

I frowned at The Bone, and he knew that in spite of the fact that I smoked with him and some of the others, I didn't like it for everyone to get too stoned on the first night of a hip shoot.

"Look," I told the Bone, "just because we're in a real nice set up doesn't mean we can get all shit-faced and everything right off the bat. You better cool it until we see what's up."

"I already know what's up, Blackie. None of us has guard and all we gotta do is be here for fire missions. Green said that as long as we stayed out of their way, we can do just about what we want."

I smirked, and The Bone took my meaning.

"Well, within reason, and this stuff is so good you're really gonna thank me for finding it for us." Someone called for him to move the truck again and before The Bone left, he flashed me the peace sign and winked.

The Bone had a knack of finding out what was going to happen. As it turned out, he was right about not having guard. Just as we were entering their bivouac, the Koreans were forming their guard mount. The big Korean sergeant, who later said "Yobo Shibo" to Big and me, was sergeant of the guard and he addressed his men in a clear, steady Korean (whatever that implies) and probably informing them that there was a heavy cloud cover and not much of a moon. It would be quite dark and therefore they would have to be doubly alert and responsive. His speech ended abruptly on a high note of dismissal. The guard mount had fallen out, fanning in all directions toward the ten or so bunkers that nestled into the hill just below the crest. The Koreans had taken many precautions around the perimeter so that the hilltop was surrounded by a continuous line of concertina, barbed wire, trip flares, empty pop cans which would rattle if touched, and whatever else they may have had that didn't show.

Our gun crew, which consisted of Lieutenant Charles, Sergeants Green and Bush, me, Louie, The Bone and four other enlisted men, made desultory arrangements for chow and sleeping, for now that we knew we had nothing more to do that night, we felt no urgency. Lieutenant Charles had spoken with the Korean commander (who was the only Korean on the hill who could speak English) who told him that as far as he was concerned, we should concentrate our entire efforts on performing well on the gun. This, according to the lieutenant, meant we could do just about what we wanted as long as we didn't interfere with the Koreans. We were in for a lot of loafing, it seemed.

I found The Bone again who, with Big and a few others, was sharing a bowl of marijuana outside of a guard bunker. As I approached, I noticed that one of the group was a Korean. The Bone handed me the bowl (a smoking pipe) and I took a turn on it, passing it on to the Korean. To my amazement, for we had heard about the strict discipline of the Koreans, he accepted the bowl and smoked it.

"Hey," I proclaimed to no one in particular, "I wonder if this guy knows he's smoking dope."

"I don't think so," Big replied. "It's sort of a dirty trick, but how the hell you gonna explain to him? And if we don't share it, he might think we're being rude or something."

I turned to the Korean soldier. He smiled at me the way it seemed they all did. He was young and he had a handsome, clear-skinned face with sort of flat nose and deeply set black eyes, not at all slanted, but almond shaped and nicely proportioned. His breath smelled like fish and rice and marijuana with maybe a subtle hint of hot pepper as well. I gathered he was on guard because he wore a flak jacket and his steel pot and M-16 were by his side. I tried not to imagine what would happen to him if he got caught. Probably not too much as long as we were here. But when we left, his commander would mete out corporal punishment, Korean style. I thought I should at least try to explain to him what he was smoking. He must have been feeling a bit funny by now. I'd only had one toke and I was already stoned. The Bone was right. This was righteous dew. I knew there were clouds covering the darkening sky, but I saw stars anyway.

"You bek, cunsai?" I asked the Korean.

"Yobo shibo!" he answered.

Big and I exchanged glances.

"Yobo shibo?" I asked.

He nodded enthusiastically, "Yobo shibo."

I crossed my arms in front of me like an umpire signaling 'safe' in a baseball game.

"No!" I said forcefully, but still smiling friendly.

"Marijuana," I explained.

Everyone laughed, and so the Korean did, too.

"He don't know marijuana," Big told me. "How could he? I'm telling you, Blackie, I tried, but he keeps on taking his turn when the bowl comes by."

"Maybe we should put it away then," I suggested.

"Yeah, dig it, man, "Big concurred. "Besides, we're all so spaced out by now it wouldn't do any good to smoke any more anyway."

"What's 'yobo shibo' mean, anyway? Is that his name or something?" asked Bone while slowly putting away his marijuana.

"Well," I said, "if it is, then there's two Koreans here that have the same name. That big sergeant said the same thing to us. I don't see why we couldn't call 'em both Yobo Shibo anyway. I mean, some people think all Orientals look alike, so why shouldn't they have the same name?" I laughed.

But no one else did because they knew that the "people" that I referred to were some of the people in our gun section who had little regard for anyone who even looked different than they did.

We sat or stood around for a while longer but we were quiet, listening to the night sounds. It was pitch black by now. The Koreans were much better at keeping quiet than we were. All there was to hear were brief phrases of English, sounds of someone's mess kit or an occasional pop-top opening. But the Koreans, except for our Yobo Shibo buddy, seemed to have melted into the night. They simply weren't around anymore. One by one the members of the small smoking party drifted off to get some sleep. I still stood next to Yobo Shibo and I watched him as he stared off into the middle distance, what we called "the Vietnam stare." He gazed for quite some time and then shook his head as if trying to shed some sort of idea or feeling. He hissed out a quick breath through clenched teeth and looked up at me wonderingly. I smiled and placed a hand on his shoulder in a friendly way.

"Cunsai," I said and turned to walk away.

"Yobo shibo," he answered in a low voice.

When we spent any length of time on a hip shoot, which was what we were on, I always brought along my mesh hammock. Usually, I could find something to tie it on so that I didn't have to crash out on the ground. I had more than the normal aversion to snakes, lizards, scorpions, slugs, and roaches and was willing to trade the relative safety of a bunker or a foxhole for an elevated sleeping position. And so I dug out my hammock and tied one end to our gun and the other to the five-ton truck which, because of the limited quarters of the hilltop, was only a few feet away. It didn't take long for me to realize how tired I was. My bones ached from the long convoy. I leaned into my hammock and reached out to give myself a little swing. Before I quit rocking, I was asleep.

Dreams revamp waking reality, warping it into their own needs, so that we rarely really know how time, or space, works in a dream. I saw myself dancing in an arena with a formation of costumed, oriental figures. We chanted while performing a ritualistic, martial arts exercise in unison. My dream came along beside me, telling me to wake up before opening my eyes. While in Vietnam, or in any combat zone, odd personal traits develop and are honed. One of mine was to wake up before opening my eyes. My dream analyzed what was happening around my hammock and manufactured a scene that would coincide with it. As the dancers in my dream performed perfectly executed leg thrusts, I woke up, keeping my eyes closed. I heard movement all around me and someone chanting, with a group responding. Slowly, I opened my eyes. The sun had just peeked above the far eastern ridge, illuminating, for my first view, the hilltop held by the Koreans. A formation of soldiers stood around me. They faced east, addressing the sun and responding to the chant of the first Yobo Shibo who Big and I had met the night before, the big Korean sergeant. With his back to the men, the sergeant led them through a series of graceful but deadly taekwondo positions. They would move in a group as if in slow motion, but then lash out with cat like speed with a hand or foot and ending the thrust in a ferocious, twisting release of pent-up energy that crackled in the early morning air. Then they would pull it all back in and move slowly through another period of controlled build-up and release. Even in my sleep-logged condition, their behavior demanded and received my fullest attention. They prayed, meditated and trained all at the same time and I began to wonder if we had come to the right hilltop. Were these soldiers? Or avatars from another realm that had come to play tricks on us "good old boys?" But then I recognized the soldier next to me, only three feet away. It was the second Yobo Shibo who had smoked with us the night before. He saw me watching him out of the corner of his eye. He winked down at me and smiled.

"Yobo shibo," he whispered.

I told him the same. It was also best, I decided, to stay in my hammock until their formation ended, not wanting to get clobbered by a Korean hand or foot turned into a lethal weapon. Finally, their big sergeant, who I decided to call Yobo Shibo the First, snapped them all to attention and drove them off to breakfast.

The Lt. and Sergeant Green came by shortly and told me to get it together for an early registration for the gun. The Korean FO (forward observer) was already in position. We began fusing rounds and arranging powder canisters, Big and Louie aligned the gun and then the Lt. and Sergeant Green put the finishing touches on. Soon we began lobbing rounds into the far end of the valley as the entire infantry company, and their commander, watched on with inspiration and awe. Our gun section had been picked for this hip shoot because we worked fast, made no mistakes, and kept the gun in perfect order. We saw that the Koreans appreciated this through their gesticulations and sound effects. They were a happy bunch, today.

After the registration we didn't have much to do so we just hung around watching how the Koreans spent their time. Their big sergeant, Yobo Shibo the First, loved taekwondo and feats of strength or competition. As we would observe throughout the following days, he spent a large portion of each day in special movements, or just plain wrestling. He even had a Charles Atlas weight set with him that he wanted his men to use. He would lift them, always adding more weight, urging his men to build themselves up. The other Yobo Shibo, who we decided to call Yobo Shibo the Second, always partook in the exercises, but somehow would remain aloof and detached. His friends didn't seem to get after him for this, though, and actually seemed to treat him differentially. We soon found out that Yobo Shibo the Second was their most experienced and effective point man, who they trusted almost reverently to lead them away from ambushes and booby traps. He led more patrols than anyone else on the hilltop and no one, including Yobo Shibo the First, tried to change his attitude.

Our Lt. wanted the gun section to maintain the right attitude by keeping busy at least some of the time. He told Sergeant Green to tell Big and the rest of us to secure the ammunition, which meant taking it off the truck and loading it into the low bunker next to the gun. After the required amount of complaining we turned to the task. Yobo Shibo the First watched, along with the others, as we all took turns hauling the one hundred seventy-five-pound projectiles from the truck the bunker. We each took one on our shoulder, except Big, who always took two, one on each shoulder. This impressed the Korean sergeant, who expressed it by pointing out Big to his men. I got the feeling that Yobo Shibo the First regarded Big as something of a work elephant or draft animal. I don't suppose that there was any way for the Koreans to know, except maybe through human instinct, that Elliot Bush possessed a rare sensitivity and that his feelings were bruised easily when seen merely as a big, strong thing. And I knew Big would guard his feelings by holding them in, and since he didn't know much about taekwondo or other forms of release and control that might help stabilize his emotions, there was trouble brewing below the horizon.

Several days passed and a certain sort of routine developed. We would conduct hundred-round fire missions throughout the entire night, firing in a syncopated rhythm. Then the Koreans would conduct patrols with one platoon that was already in position from the night ambushes and another, fresh platoon that would move out from the hilltop. A third platoon would set out listening posts in the evening while the remaining platoon would pull security for the gun. It all ran in an orderly and seemingly predictable manner. We all knew that the Cong watched us all the time, but I doubt that even they, with their "home field advantage," knew where we would target for the night, or where the Koreans would operate in the valley. No matter what patterns were used, however, the Koreans did not succeed in drawing out any Cong of more than squad strength. Perhaps the Koreans should have known how things were to be . . . by analyzing the way they had taken the hill. On the morning they took the hill they simply walked to the top to find that it had been evacuated during the night. The Cong had known that they couldn't hold out forever, so they cut loose, either to make use of another valley to run supplies through, or to play cat and mouse with the Koreans. The latter of the two seemed more realistic and in keeping, for the Koreans had a reputation for evil doings in the bush and usually the Cong preferred to give them their distance. They reasoned, perhaps, that even though the Koreans were effective, they were sparse, so let them be. The valley would always be there after the Koreans withdrew. Besides, for every Korean unit in Vietnam, there was one less for the communists in Korea to contend with, so, for the Cong, it was a matter of six of one and a half dozen of the other.

The Koreans were there for one set of reasons, while the Cong left them alone for another entirely different set of reasons. I came to learn this in a roundabout way after only a few days of the hip shoot. The Koreans, besides staying physically fit, practiced a mental game as well. They called it Gomiko. I saw them playing this game quite often and, unlike the rest of the gun crew, knew exactly what it was, for it was an elementary version of an oriental game I learned back in the World. Two players alternated placing either black or white stones (one played black, one white) on the intersections of a grid with nineteen horizontal and nineteen vertical lines. Once a stone was played it could not be moved. The object of the game was to place five of your stones in a horizontal, vertical or diagonal row before the other player did. It required placements that served defensive as well as offensive purposes and the Koreans were quit adept at filling up the entire board with no one stringing out five in a row. Some of our gun crew learned Gomiko and one even did quite well against the more inexperienced Koreans, holding out for as many as twenty moves before succumbing. I, although extremely interested in their game, never played, or expressed much of an interest in it, choosing, instead, to observe candidly from a distance in order to see which of the Koreans played with the most skill. I had plans, for the game that I had in mind was the ancient Chinese, and later, Japanese game of Go, which is to Gomiko as chess is to checkers. I chose to remain a dark horse, in the event that The Bone, who saw in the Koreans an opportunity to fleece in gambling, could set up a match later on. It was the Korean's preoccupation with Gomiko that pointed out the difference between their war strategy and the Cong's strategy. While the Koreans were interested in developing and infusing the strategies of Gomiko, the Cong, it seemed to me, were more interested in developing the strategies of Go.

In another sense, our involvement in the war, and to a lesser extent the Korean's involvement, fit this pattern. Put simply, we were conducting a different sort of strategy than were the Cong and therefore we had a different understanding of what really was happening. Our "victories" were shallow while their "defeats" were not significant because our goals were not the same as the goals of the Cong. If the Cong declined to contact the Koreans, it didn't signify a defeat, or a diminishing of their will, but rather it signified a reality quite separate from what the Koreans and, in a broader sense, the Americans considered important. In the long run, however, perhaps it is the intangible elements of a war that makes it the ultimate evil that it is. It is the lonely soldier crawling through the mud that realizes that the insecurity spawned by the devil and the chaotic void is what drives people to kill and rape and destroy. The devil knows his subjects well and knows what tunes to pipe so that humanity will dance the dance of death. I think that among all the Koreans on the hilltop, only Yobo Shibo the Second felt the dance of death, and felt its horrid rhythm seeping through the soles of his boots to quake his body, on occasion, and come to rest behind his distant eyes.

As it turned out, there were very few Cong in the valley. After ten days of working over the valley with high explosives and patrols and ambushes, the Koreans only turned up a small medical cache and an alternative route to the Ho Chi Minh Trail. But none of us considered the time ill spent, at least no one in our gun section did. After all, it stood for ten less days left in our tour and besides, we made friends with the Koreans. Even though I thought they had missed the boat concerning what was really happening in this war, I saw them as another slice of life, adding to the flavor of the population of the world. Yobo Shibo the First still kept taunting Big, though, and maybe because he actually did understand that Big was sensitive and didn't like it. Perhaps all of this would have come to naught if The Bone hadn't seen in it another opportunity to fleece the Koreans. Yobo Shibo the First and the Koreans, even though observing Big accomplish great feats of strength, really had no idea whatsoever as to his real power. They had never seen him tip a jeep on its side so we could work on it. They had never seen him handle the eight-inch rounds, which weighed two hundred pounds, with as much ease as the 175mm rounds. This is why The Bone pursued the possibility of a match between Big and Yobo Shibo the First, along with a match between their best Gomiko player and me, the dark horse.

On the day before we were to leave, The Bone, through monumental efforts that taxed his fast-talking skills to the limit, was able to round up some beer from the village below as well as talk our Lt. into convincing the Korean commander that a little celebration and entertainment would be a good thing. It would revive the esprit de corps and also, The Bone confided to our Lt., we could stand to make a few bucks from the Koreans. Our Lt. was no slouch, and he was all in favor of returning to our firebase in high spirits. He also knew of Big's hidden power and so was intrigued with the possibility of a match on which to bet Big against the Korean.

I had my doubts, both about Big and myself. I knew Big's hidden strength, but I also knew his hidden weakness. He wasn't a fighter, and he wasn't very coordinated. Yobo Shibo the First had been egging him on ever since we arrived, demonstrating that he indeed was a fighter. He was also lightning fast, with reflexes which sprang from natural coordination. Only if The Bone could devise the right sort of match would Big really have much of a chance. The Bone rose to the challenge, convincing the Koreans, with a diagram drawn in the sand with a hyperbole of body language, that the best match possible would combine Japanese Sumo wrestling with throwing your opponent over. A big round ring would be drawn in the dirt. If you could push your opponent out of the ring without ending out of the ring yourself, then you won. Because of the size difference, the bone gave odds to the Koreans. For every two dollars they put in, we would put in three. I still had my doubts.

I didn't know if I really could get the best of their best Gomiko player. He played with a style that I couldn't decipher, but the Bone enticed them into an all or nothing match. We were to play only one game. The Bone and I considered this to my advantage, for if I could sente (gain advantage) him right away, I had a better chance of winning. The Bone was able to bring the odds back to even by insisting that the Koreans put up three dollars to every two of ours. The Lt. would hold the Korean money and the Korean commander would hold ours. Perhaps the Koreans were becoming a bit suspicious now, but The Bone was operating in his true element and was able to regain their confidence with more hyperbole and a great amount of toothy grinning.

Big's desire and my ability bugged me, but the Koreans held our money, and they were in a festive mood. They allowed themselves to feel intoxicated, even though their commander had rationed out beer so that each can had to be shared between two men. They would share their beer as longtime friends or loving brothers would, pleased to have any at all, rather than disgusted because they only had half a can each. The beer went to their heads immediately. Some of them started singing and one or two even began stumbling around as if in a blackout. But Yobo Shibo the First, who took no ration of beer, stood out above them all, arms akimbo, wearing a determined yet whimsical expression. Our gun section mixed in with the Koreans, and I looked for Big.

It didn't take long to see that he wasn't around. But I wanted to talk with him before the contests began. I found him leaning up against a bunker, tossing pebbles into the concertina at a "fuck you" lizard.

"Fuck you! Fuck you!" the lizard said.

Big didn't answer.

"Hey, Big," I announced, "how ya' doin'?"

He shrugged his shoulders, saying it all wordlessly.

I sat down with him. "I better cut through all the bullshit and get to the point since we don't have much time."

He looked at me, knitting his brows.

"I know you feel like you're put up to this, Big, and I'm going to let The Bone have it when we get out of here. If I didn't know him better, I'd say he's acting like a pimp, but he's been pretty faithful to the gun section, and he does a lot for us that no one else could do. You know?"

Big nodded, tossing another pebble at the lizard.

"Fuck you!" the lizard said.

"But you know, Elliot? I think you can take Yobo Shibo without anyone even getting a scratch."

Big turned to face me again, letting his eyes ask how.

"You see, it's like this. He's gonna try to use your strength against you to sort of throw you over. It's sort of the way the Cong conduct this war, if you know what I mean."

Big sat up a little and dispersed the lizard with his hand full of pebbles. The lizard careened down the slope and disappeared over the edge of a rock.

"Tell me more, Blackie. I mean, I don't want to fight 'em, but since that asshole The Bone went and set everything up, I figure the best way to do it would be to let Yobo Shibo wear himself out. I really don't think he could move me if I don't move first."

"There it is, Big. He's quick and everything, but I really don't think he's too smart. I get the feeling that he thinks you're dumb or something and will try to come at him with everything at once. If you do, you've had it. You'll be on your back or out of the ring before you can blink your eyes. But if you're coy and make him come to you, well, you know better than me what you can do if you get the right grip on him."

"Where do you think I should get a grip on him, Blackie?"

"Well, I don't know, for sure, but maybe not around his hands or lower arms. I think he could break even your grip with the right kind of quickness and leverage. He might even break you are arm if you try that. But if you can latch on to him up around his shoulders or upper body, then you can press your advantage for what I think is your best bet."

"What's that?' Big asked.

"You have to get him off the ground and just walk him right out of the ring. The Koreans will freak out!"

Big stood up, listening to the maniacal screams of the Koreans who were now being joined by our gun section in the celebration. We could tell that the whole bunch were loose and looking for entertainment.

"Why don't you stay here for a while, Big, while I go play the Korean in Gomiko. You need to think this out a little more, on your own and besides, my match shouldn't take long, either way."

Big agreed and I went off to find their best Gomiko player. He was the oldest Korean on the hilltop. Maybe forty. He had already set out his board, with the black stones (which played first) in a small bowl next to where I was to sit. There were a few other Koreans sitting around him, non-drinkers, I assumed, and Sergeant Green and the Lt. were there, too. I was glad for their support.

The Korean politely pointed for me to sit and begin. I didn't play coy. I played the best point, which was the exact center of the board, and I played with the authority that my Go teacher had taught me. The stone snapped on the board, and I withdrew my hand to replace it in my lap. I sat on the ground, cross-legged, with my back held in a straight up and down, yogic position. His response combined defense with offense by positioning a stone adjacent to mine on a diagonal line. I offset his play by also playing on the diagonal, one down and one to the left of my first stone. This accomplished two things. First, I cut off his horizontal prospects and second it gave me two in a row as well as the start of a cluster. Half of the winning strategy in Gomiko, as with most games of its type, considers your opponent's response to your own moves. You have to realize that if you start clustering, your opponent, in order to stay in the game, must necessarily respond by playing what first appears to be isolated stones on the edge of your cluster. But, as the game advances, his seemingly isolated stones begin to develop into threats. The Korean didn't respond to my cluster, and I guessed he believed me to be shortsighted. I engaged his second stone by blocking his vertical line from above while at the same time extending my row to three on the diagonal, with two open ends. This forced him to play far out on the fringe in order to keep me from winning. If he hadn't, I merely would have needed to play one more in the line, then, unhindered, a fifth.

It was at this point where many of my friends had gone wrong. They failed to recognize the threat from an open-ended three and, instead of defending against the threat, would play a strictly offensive point in an isolated area. But obviously the Korean recognized the threat and responded. I then played on the point one below and one to the right of dead center, which caught him off guard, for it was a double attack that only an expert player would try. He sat up, issued a short grunt, looking at me with a bit of suspicion. Unless he were to hustle, now, his previously nonchalant attitude would spell defeat for him and, more importantly, I'm sure he felt, for Korea. But instead of analyzing the situation so as to respond adequately, which he still could have done, he played a brash and foppish point, instead, by adding a stone to a closed two. This left me open to develop my double attack even farther, which I did eventually play, but only after a short period in which I let him think I was hesitant and unsure of just what to do next. When I finally did play on the one point that would lead to dangerous repercussions, he breathed in with a quick, short breath, then let out with somewhat of an international sound of recognition. I had broken him in five moves by building a strong offense while leaving him with only scattered and isolated points on the board.

The game was over on the eleventh point. Sergeant Green and the Lt. didn't realize it until the Korean and his friends got up rather briskly, mumbling to themselves and shaking their heads.

"Did you win, or something?" Sergeant Green asked.

"There it is." I replied, pointing to my open-ended four, which was impossible to defend.

"You and The Bone had this all figured out, didn't you?" Asked the Lt. with a mixture of disgust and pleasure in his tone.

"Dig it, sir," I said.

They walked off together toward the group of howling men, shaking their heads.

"That's diabolical." I heard one of them say.

Both the Koreans and our gun section howled and cavorted around the edge of the rings drawn in the red dirt. They wanted action, now that the beer was gone. The Bone moved through the crowd like a bee busy pollinating flowers. When I reached the circle, I caught his eye and motioned for him to come over.

"I took the Korean."

"Yeah, I know," he replied. "They ain't too happy 'bout it either. They think they was framed. Hah!"

"Did you collect, Bone?"

"Nah, not yet. I been too busy keeping everybody piped down." He looked the crowd over. "Where's Big, anyway? You seen him, Blackie?"

"Yeah, yeah. He'll be here. He's just psyching up. And thinking about what he's gonna do to you when we get back to the firebase."

The Bone stared at me in mock disbelief and was about to defend himself when we saw Big approaching the crowd. He walked right through them to stand in the center of the ring. Yobo Shibo the First joined him. They both had taken their shirts off and each were beginning to sweat in the heat of the noon day sun. The Bone broke off his discussion with me and hurried to join the two in the ring. He stood between them and in his best New Jersey accent he began.

"Ladies 'n gentlemen. Da followin' exhibition is a sorta' combination a sumo rasslin' an' street brawl."

The GIs laughed and the Koreans followed their lead.

"On my right's Sergeant Yobo Shibo da Foist . . ."

The Bone pointed to the big sergeant as he spoke and the Korean's got a big charge out of hearing their champion called 'Yobo Shibo,' but they weren't about to tell us what it meant.

"Weighin' in at about one hunnert ninety pounds, soakin' wet!"

Then The Bone turned to Big. "An' on my left is Big, weighin' in at two-forty." He held up his hand to try to quiet down the excited and somewhat intoxicated crowd. "Da rules is ta push da udder guy out a da soikle widout yerself leavin' it, or knocks da udder guy down by trippin' or shovin', or to make da udder guy wanna quit. Is dat understood by the contestants?"

Big nodded. The Korean, not knowing a word of English, just stood there, waiting for the match to begin.

"Okay, den. Do it!"

The crowd backed off to give them their distance. The ring opened to a forty-foot diameter, giving the Korean plenty of room to maneuver, which everyone soon realized was his plan. He darted in and out, trying to draw Big off guard or off balance so as to utilize Big's strength, size and momentum to throw him down or push him out of the ring. Big moved extraordinarily slow and with a controlled pace. He held his hands loosely at his sides. He kept allowing Yobo Shibo the First to close on him quickly. The Korean would try a trip step or some other sort of in-maneuvering designed to draw Big off balance. But Big kept his center of gravity very low, although he appeared to be unable to respond quickly enough to Yobo Shibo's sorties. Big started breathing heavy and The Bone gave me a worried look from across the circle. Big kept his eyes wide open and tightly focused on the Korean's stomach as he slowly circled clockwise for a round or two and then counterclockwise. The Koreans urged their sergeant on, obliging him to put an end to the match so they could get back the money they lost in the Gomiko match and so they could be proud again.

The guys in our gun section were confused by Big's tactics. Louie wanted to know why Big didn't just run up to that little shit and throw him away. I suggested that Yobo Shibo wasn't as small as they thought he was. Big kept circling, though, and soon Yobo Shibo, who was in excellent condition, began to tire some and waver ever so slightly. Big noticed. He crouched even deeper, presenting an even lower profile than the Korean. His breathing leveled into long, slow, controlled breaths. The Koreans reassessed the situation and their frolicking gestures turned into more of a study of turning the tide.

"Keep circling, Big!" I yelled.

As yet, Big hadn't raised his hands above his waste and Yobo Shibo must have grown used to it. The pressure from his mates, frustration and exertion of a second and third wind finally drew him off-sides just an inch too far. Big's right hand came across from above and behind Yobo Shibo the First, latching, like a railroad coupling, into his shoulder. He let out a yell and his knees buckled. He was in pain, and it told instantly in his face, but Yobo Shibo was no punk. His buckling knees suddenly turned into a springboard that he used to twist away from Big. But as he twisted, Big slipped his reserved left hand between Yobo Shibo's driving legs. Big held him at arm's length, squatted slightly and then stood up straight, jerking Yobo Shibo straight up over his head.

And then silence. We all waited for Big to decide what he would do with Yobo Shibo. And in that silence, many of our lives were saved. We all heard the mortar rounds come whistling in and in that milli-second that stands between recognition and reaction, we all pretty much summed the whole thing up. We represented a target that no self-respecting Cong could disregard. On top of it all, I figured out later, our drawing fire was obviously no ploy, for we had no one to mark the origin of the rounds.

The first round landed about as close as any first round could. But, having heard it in that brief moment of silence, we all hit the ground, including Big and Yobo Shibo the First. But the second round broke us up like a cue ball on a fresh rack, hurling a leg and an arm through the air and over our heads. We were bracketed. And why not? The Cong had held this hill, off and on, for years and it was now obvious that they knew every range coordinate by heart. It seemed that they were working out on us with only one mortar, taking time to adjust between rounds. A third round came in, detonating in some B-40 mesh and we all took off, heading for bunkers or to bring our gun to bear, if possible. But the Cong are masters of psychological warfare. Instead of laying it on us, they cut it off as quickly as it had started, high tailing it to fight another day.

It was a bad scene. Laments, screams, medics shaking their heads, everything that reviles and then remains as a recurring little drama which replays on its own. The casualties dwell in the coffers of an emotional top secret. High priority, for eyes (or vision) only. All that good military stuff. The party was over. All bets off. The Koreans bought more that day than we did. I guess it was because there were more of them there to buy it. One of the three rounds, the second one, was a direct hit on Yobo Shibo the Second. Maybe it was punishment for smoking dope (even though he never knew it) with the Americans. Well, he never knew his punishment, either.

the White Horse Division

you join them at Song Mao,
the White Horse Division from the Republic of Korea,
every night they take prisoners, who always die at first
light,
when the Cong return to the rice paddies, and the NVA
lies low,
every day you watch the Koreans,
they do not smoke marijuana, they do not drink beer,
at sunrise, they practice taekwondo,
at sundown, they meditate,
like monks honing their desire
for the next mission

the Kuomintang

you get old in the 'Nam
but not as old as the Kuomintang
you watch them from inside the tree line
they carry dated weapons, their uniforms faded and
patched
they gather around their cooking fires
the gray ones standing in the monsoon, waiting to move
on
the last vestige of Sun Yat-Sen

the accords

admit nothing
deny everything
make counter accusations
let god sort them out

Wes

you drop out of college
you're good for basic
good for infantry training, and then OCS
you come to the 'Nam as a butter bar
but second lieutenants die fast in the 'Nam
ambush, AK-47, sucking chest wound
you go home in a bag
your wife never meets you
your children are never born
and your only contribution is your death

Wayne

you stutter
you have few friends, but your family loves you
you graduate low, and your lottery number is lower
you end up driving a jeep in the 'Nam
you drive over a mine
lose both eyes, and your left arm
they send you home without them
it takes so long for you to die
and your name never appears on the Wall
only here

A week after Young returned from R&R I pulled guard with him. We had come in-country at about the same time, and we were now two of the more senior members of a 105mm howitzer battery. We were assigned to our favorite bunker for guard. It overlooked the steep side of the hill which our firebase, named after the West Point captain who was killed in action on the hilltop while trying to lay the battery. For the last two weeks an infantry company had been operating in the valley, pulling patrols during the day and setting ambushes or listening posts at night. But now their commander had pulled the company together around our guns, just outside the perimeter. Young and I felt that, even though no one can really tell, this night would pass in relatively safe non-activity and without too much responsibility for us to deal with.

You could say that Young and I were close friends. We both came from the same state, which usually generated a sort of tacit understanding, depending on how big a state you came from. Also, we both had some university experience, having majored in liberal arts. We talked a lot about books and ideas and history. We talked about being drafted, since that was what we both had been, and how it all came about. On several occasions, after long nights on guard, we agreed that perhaps the only currently evident reason for us having allowed ourselves to be drafted and caught up in the war was to try out the marijuana. As civilians we had been hippies or were trying to be. We heard plenty about how potent the marijuana was in 'Nam and how cheaply it could be attained. This admission about drugs made us think about their influence on us. It was scary. Unknown authorities always told us of habituation and dependency but, like most young people, we thought they were talking about somebody else. Now, the thought that perhaps our dependency, maybe a psychological dependency, had helped create our present situation, dwelled in the back of our minds. This perplexed and, in a way, haunted us both.

Lately Young talked about Australia and I listened because I was scheduled for R&R in a week. He always got around to talking about tripping on acid and when he showed us the LSD that he had brought back we knew what he had in mind. I guess some of us always seemed to talk about it, but we never had any of it around, until now. We worried about the consequences. What would happen if some of us were tripping and then it got hot? Our present situation reminded us of an indefinite sort of "American Roulette," played for a year and probably never forgotten. Would the odds change if we were to introduce psychedelic, hallucinatory drugs into the karmic stew? Well, we just didn't know, except that if it were to happen, we knew it would have to be a group effort.

I felt, on my way to the guard bunker, that if Young was planning to try out any of his LSD on us, it would be tonight. I made it to the bunker first and started setting up claymore mines and the M-60 machine gun. I set out hand flares in a handy place and generally squared everything away. I sat back, taking in the valley below. The area below the bunker was a free fire zone and an infantry squad, which was digging in just off to the right, made sure to stay out of our field of fire. I could hear them talking casually among themselves. They seemed relaxed and I knew it was because they were out of the heavy bush for the night.

"Crap," I heard one of them remark, "I wish I was in the artillery. They've got it made. They never, but fucking never, have to hump the bush. They even got cots to sleep in!"

I reflected on this for a moment. Everything's relative, I deduced. Many times, when we returned to base camp, we complained about how headquarters had it made. They had showers! And movies at night. And a real mess hall, if that was any consolation. The base camp personnel would look at us as if we were aliens from another world when we would convoy in after being ambushed on the road, after losing friends in a firefight. The last firefight came to mind without any prompting. Unrelated elements of that ambush drew together like metal filings to a magnet, and I was reviewing the rocketed two-and-a-half-ton truck, full of ARVN troops. Traffic backed up; civilian vehicles mixed in with military vehicles. People screamed in Vietnamese and English. Blood dripped from the burning truck. The villagers gawking, scurrying, wandering, visiting, conducting business, accepting it all as a way of life for them. I looked out over the M-60 machine gun I sat behind and I saw the switchback road. One side dropped off steeply, falling away purposefully to the coastal plane and Phan Rang, our destination. The other side rose steeply; above I saw part of the same road we were on now. Someone had called in artillery rounds, and we all watched as they whooshed in, landing two hundred meters beyond the ambush. Who called in those rounds? Were they supposed to be friendly? Someone was walking them in on us and now there was more screaming. Our lieutenant told me to dismount the M-60 and set up in sort of an alley or ditch, facing the road. He joined me, ready to assist me.

It's so bizarre, I remember thinking. Here we are, waiting to maybe kill somebody and yet some of the Vietnamese are waiting for traffic to clear so they can get on with business.

"At least I don't have to worry 'bout being drafted and gettin' sent to 'Nam." It was the grunts below, digging in for the night, who brought me back to the here and now. I laughed. I liked the grunts for their sense of humor, diabolical as it always was.

From above the bunker, I heard Young call down to me.

"Hey Longstreet! Are you down there?"

I told him I was. He same down the steps and into the bunker, scraping his M-16 and grenade launcher against the narrow walls as he came. He bumped his helmet against the overhead beam and his flak jacket caught on a spike that we used for hanging equipment. He sighed, unhooked himself and began making his own little arrangements so as to know where things were and have them within reach when it was dark. The sun balanced on the hilltops across the valley. The long, refracted angle of the sun produced red light. Heat waves above the brown ridge line caused the sun to waver, as if it were a hallucination. The deep green of the valley floor turned black. I thought of the grunts and how pleased they were not to be down there tonight. A few Vietnamese, farmers and kids, came up the trails leading out of the valley. They carried produce and a collection of unidentifiable objects, all hanging from poles and counterbalanced across their shoulders. This scene is a thousand years old, I thought. Some drove water buffalo ahead of them with a child or two riding on the backs of the obliging beasts. As they approached, the buffs would flair their wide nostrils and look around in wild-eyed warning. They smelled GIs.

After a few gentle whacks on their backsides the buffs would move on. The farmers were tired and wanted to get home. Besides, there was a curfew. The infantry unit, part of which was dug in below us, had been operating in this area and had taken a few prisoners lately, killing one or two as it turned out, who did not want to be prisoners, or so it seemed. Relations with the village had never been good. Heavy handedness, although common as rain, never went down well. And then there was the artillery with its constant fire mission, chewing up the valley and fertilizing their fields with shrapnel. But these people were peasants, poor people to the GIs. They had no recourse to the destruction except more endless hard work as well as a sort of patience which emanated from the local Buddhist shrine.

"You know?" Young began philosophically. "This valley could be a veritable paradise." He shook his head slowly, indicating, I guessed, that he understood the history of the valley. I thought to myself that the next thing he would say was, it's a shame.

"It's a shame," he went on, "a fucking shame. Have you ever seen that waterfall up in the valley wall north of here?"

He pointed to where it would be. "The 'Yards" (by this he meant the Montagnards) "have a tiny village up there, out of our range. I've been up there a few times. Man, it's elegant, in a primitive sort of way. I mean, they have elephants up there that they use to haul down logs for market. I think it's teakwood. I'd like to come back here someday, when it's all over, and just live in this valley for a while. The 'Yards are fine people. They're so honest. Don't you think so?"

Young was a little romantic at times, but I agreed with him anyway because he was my friend, and besides, I figured he was right about the Montagnards. They were honest, at least more honest than anyone else I'd dealt with lately, and I had romantic notions about them too. They lived nearer to the hub in the wheel of God, or Buddha, or whatever you might call it. The Great Everywhere Spirit, I guess. I always believed romanticism would outlive reality. The Montagnards gave me a spiritual feeling and that is something every GI needs in order to survive emotionally.

"They're such good, humble people. And now they're without a home and nobody gives a shit. We give them weapons when they want peace, and we stay when they don't want us, and they can't stand the Vietnamese either."

Young was gearing up for one of his famous monologues concerning the nature of things.

"And so, the chaplain says life ain't perfect and we gotta bear up under our cross. Well shit, I don't know much about the Bible, but I knew Jesus Christ didn't have all this crap in mind when he was bearing his cross. Christ must have a hell of a karma."

Young was about to hit high gear and I really didn't want to listen to it all again.

"You know? Sometimes I really wonder about karma," he went on. "I mean, sometimes I wonder if it's not just another shell game. And if it is . . ."

"Young," I interrupted, "have you ever tried Japanese flower arranging?"

He looked over at me, squinting one eye to let me sort of know that he knew I wasn't serious. He sat back and went for a while without talking, watching the sun go down. The stars, by one and then by twos and threes started shining, some brightly, and some not. Soon there was an infinite number of stars, an infinity for every soldier ever made. Or, I wondered, are soldiers born? For some reason I remembered what Young had brought back from Sydney. He had referred to it as a gift for us, and one of the ex-hippies in our gun section was interested, a guy we called Hammurabi. If Hammurabi were to show tonight while Young and I were on guard, I believed we'd have a go at it. This was the night for it.

All of the elements were in place, it seemed, and we felt that we were doing something unique, that we were conducting some sort of exotic experiment. Our egos fed us. Thousands of millions have gone to war. Quite a few have done psychedelics. But how many have combined the two? Maybe some spear carrying natives of the Amazon and perhaps a few Nazi officers; that's about it. So why not give it a whirl? We agreed. What have we got to lose? We asked.

What have we got to lose; I was wondering as Hammurabi announced himself from above the bunker. He was off guard, he told us, and wanted to see what we were up to. Hammurabi liked drugs. His stocky, six-foot two-inch frame handled them well. Even in the dusk I could see his large, smiling and curious eyes prying out our intentions. His mustache drooped around the corners of his well-shaped mouth and his light brown, sun bleached hair curled over his somewhat large ears. He wore a few strings of beds around his neck and a peace medallion swung from beneath his campaign shirt.

"You look like you're waiting for the plane to take off," I said.

"Trevor," Hammurabi replied, "we're all waitin' to take off." Then he turned to Young. "Ain't that right, Leon?"

"There it is, Ham. It's about time." Young pulled out the medicine bottle that held the LSD. Six chips of "windowpane" rattled around inside.

"How strong is this stuff?" I asked.

Young leaned back, propping his boots up on the firing platform in front of us. "Well, how much of this have you ever really done, Trevor? Be honest now, 'cause I'll dose you accordingly."

I thought about it and realized that I really didn't know. It wasn't that many times that I'd tripped back in the World, but enough so that I didn't know for sure.

"Maybe a dozen times, I guess. I don't think I ever really came down all the way from that first time, though."

Young made his face take on a look of understanding.

"How 'bout you, Ham? You done this much back in the World?"

Hammurabi was quick to reply. "Well, Leon, it's like this. I don't really know, either. It's hard to say. More than once, less than twenty."

"So how strong is it?" I asked again.

"Oh, I don't know," Young said.

"What do you mean, you don't know? You're the one who took some of this, aren't you?" Hammurabi wanted to know.

"Sure. So how strong was the acid you guys took?"

I thought a moment and admitted that I didn't exactly know, except that it was very active stuff.

"Well, there it is, then. This stuff is very active, too. I just wanted to sort of see where your heads were at, I guess. Let's put it this way, these chips are strong and they're pure. No speed. No strychnine. Just LSD. I think we should each take one hit and then wait and see."

Young sat up straight, cleared his throat, and regathered our attention.

"Look, I've known you guys for half a year now. Over here that's a long time. When I decided to bring this stuff back here, I was thinking that maybe us three would be the ones to do it. I know some other guys are trying in out over here, but not that many. I think more of us should. It'll freak out the lifers. Maybe it'll shorten up this fuckin' war if they find out that a bunch of acid freaks are roaming around in the 'Nam. We got ourselves into this mess. I mean, sure, we were drafted and everything, but maybe it takes more guts to say no to something you know in your heart is wrong than it does to sort of go with the flow, or maybe with the draft, if you can dig what I'm saying. And maybe it takes guts to eat some acid when you know that the shit could hit the fan. Maybe it's insane. Sometimes I wonder if there's much difference between guts and insanity. All I know is I don't exactly want to trip alone, and I trust you guys. Do you trust me?"

"Dig it, man!" Hammurabi and I answered together.

"Well then," Young went on, "let's quick fucking around and get on with it!"

He opened the bottle and tapped three chips into his hand.

"Here, take one each and call me in the morning." We laughed. "Put it under your tongues, like where your mother always took your temperature."

"My mother always stuck it up my ass," Hammurabi explained.

"Oh, you could do that, too. It's all a matter of getting it into your bloodstream as fast as you can, you see, and the skin, or membrane under your tongue is real thin so the acid gets through it fast and into the capillaries. And then, watch out, mind!"

We sat watching each other. Then Young plopped his chip into his mouth like he was taking some snuff. He smiled.

"You know?" he said, "there's a real rush right after you drop it. I guess it's psychological because it doesn't work that fast."

"I can dig it, Leon," Hammurabi said as he took his own chip, "it's like you bought your ticket and now you're strapped into a roller coaster seat, just waiting for the ride to begin."

I took a long, deep breath, placed the translucent chip on the tip of my index finger and placed it under my tongue. The roller coaster started rolling. It was quiet now on the firebase. In the bunker where we sat, night had fallen. Beyond the hills to the west the sun still left a bit of light, but it was evaporating rapidly. It's going to be a long night, I thought to myself.

In the next half hour of silence all of Vietnam grew pitch, black dark. A few village lights burned, glowing and then dimming, subject to the whims of the generators the ARVNs guarded. All of the stars of the cosmos seemed to be peering into our bunker this evening, very bright and constant. The Vietnamese earth sucked it all up, giving back nothing. My stomach felt a little queasy so I stepped outside. After stumbling around for what seemed a long time I found myself about thirty feet from the bunker, standing in front of the star-light scope. The LSD, slowly at first but now in leaps and bounds, took over a great deal of my analysis of perception. It began as a body thing. My fingertips alternated between numbness and tingling. My lungs did funny things and so did my heart.

"Longstreet," I mumbled softly, "don't forget to breathe, or make your heartbeat."

The star-light scope stood on a tripod. It reminded me of an old studio camera because it had a canvas blackout veil you could use to keep out ground light. Beneath the veil you looked through a pair of high-powered binoculars that somehow were able to turn any available light into a weird, green panorama of what was in front of you. For the would-be hippies in the battery, the star-light scope was a favorite toy. I popped under the veil and focused on what we called the old mansion, which was set on a small hilltop about two hundred meters away. Over the last twenty-five years or so of warfare it had been razed to its foundations with the exception of a few abutments. For the last two weeks the infantry had been setting out ambushes there because we always seemed to take incoming rounds from that area. I gazed for a while; nothing there. I swung the scope slowly through the valley floor, focusing on another spot that seemed to be a desired location from which the Cong lobbed mortar rounds as us; nothing. That was the thing about the star-light scope. There was never anything to see. And if you did see anything, it usually meant something was wrong. It always gave access to another world, though, at least for a while. It was a limbo environment, neither here nor there, distantly quiet and troubled. It was the way I imagined aliens from another planet must view the world. The war always looked like it was over when I watched things through the star-light scope. Everything had been killed and demolished and destroyed. There was nothing left to fight over, and no one left to fight over it. Peace: the total absence of life. Tonight, Longstreet thought to himself, the star-light scope served as a preview of death, not his death, but the death of Earth. Being almost surely destroyed himself nearly traumatized Longstreet at times. His memory would collect the near misses, on occasion, and deposit them on the threshold of his consciousness as perhaps a nagging wife might dredge up all of the old arguments from time to time. What about the time you and Vanderveld almost rolled off the switchback with five tons of 105 shells in the truck? What about the time that idiot sergeant, (what was his name, Rawicz?) almost blew you up with his own, 'I didn't know it was loaded' grenade launcher? What about the time . . . forget it, man.

I don't know how long I had been standing out there next to the star-light scope, but I finally heard Hammurabi call out my name from the entrance of the guard bunker.

"Trevor? Come down here, man. If you're tripping like we are you probably need some company."

"Yeah, you're right, Ham. I sort of got off on a tangent, you know?"

"There it is."

When we were all sitting down again in the bunker Young asked me what I'd been doing. I told them about the star-light scope and about the near misses.

"I can dig that, man," Young responded, "but you know what freaks me out just as much? It's all those times that I really don't know about. I mean, I've seen rounds hit where guys were standin' only two minutes before. And they'd never know about it. I get to wondering how much that happens to me. It's like being stalked by some sort of karmic force. When will your luck run out?"

"They say you never hear the one that gets you," Hammurabi added as he lit a bowl of marijuana, "but I don't know if that's always the case." He passed the bowl to Young. "There're so many ways of dying over here. Some are slow. Some don't make any sound at all."

We all sat in silence for a time. At night, the lack of noise causes a vacuum that tries to suck your brains out through your ears. It gets so dark the vacuum sucks your brains out through your eyes. I felt it happening, and I wanted to talk.

"What time is it?" I asked.

I saw the radium coated dial of Young's watch float to his face. He said it was eleven.

This wasn't quite enough stimulation, so I asked them if they were high. They both snickered. Young started to giggle and then I did too. Hammurabi asked what was so funny.

"Everything's so fuckin' weird that if I don't laugh I'm gonna loose it," Young explained.

I prepared another bowl of marijuana and passed it around. I thought maybe it would calm us down even though all we were doing was sitting quietly in the dark.

"Well," Hammurabi suggested, "here we are performing our duty, which is to guard the interests and property of the United States against the forces of darkness. Sure is dark."

Young and I tried to stifle our laughter but didn't contain it very well.

"What the hell you say that for, Ham?" I asked.

"Oh, I don't know. I didn't know it was that funny. Sorry."

"No sweat, man. I think we could use a laugh." Young moved around a bit. I had the impression he was about to dive into one of his monologues.

"What's up, Leon?" I asked.

"Oh, I don't know. I was just thinkin' about acid, about what it is."

"What is it?" Hammurabi asked.

"I remember a book I read once that said you could find the active ingredients of it in ergot, which is smut that's on diseased grain, like wheat. It's an organic compound that's been around for a long time. The book suggested that back in the Middle Ages every once in a while, a whole village would go on a big acid trip because they'd all have to eat bad grain. I mean, a village couldn't just go to the grocery store to get more grain because there wasn't any more. All they could do was eat what they had and they didn't know a thing about what the smut had in it and even if they did they'd still have to eat it anyway."

I thought about what that would be like, an entire, dark age, superstition-cursed village tripping out on acid, wondering if they had all lost their minds.

Young continued. "The book wondered if maybe some of the visions that the villagers had that were blamed on the devil might not really have been drug-induced hallucinations caused by eating bad bread. Only the village alchemist would know what was happening and do you think he'd tell anybody?

"And so," Young went on, "a few nights ago I got to thinking about what it would be like if some GI brought back about a hundred hits of acid from R&R and got one of the cooks to mix it in with the fucking coffee or something. Zap! Right back to the Middle Ages. The chaplains would have a field day. Can you imagine what the battery commander would do?"

"He drinks a hell of a lot of coffee," Hammurabi reminded us.

"There it is."

We were quiet for a while. I tried to imagine what this firebase would be like if everyone felt the way we did now and didn't even know why. I kept giggling to myself. Only the acid freaks would have it together. We'd have to take command because everyone else would be running around screaming and holding their heads and staring at their hands and afraid, afraid, afraid. It's like the dark ages here, anyway, I thought, what with the fear and the suspicion. Ignorance reigns. How can this be any different than a crusade? How is this crusade any different than the ones conducted during the dark ages? No, it's different, but only in terms of technology. It's only a different crusade slugging it out through a new dark age.

Hammurabi wanted to know something. "Do you think that the Cong know anything about LSD? I mean, do you suppose they've ever considered contaminating the water supply with acid or flooding the black-market with it?"

I told him that I already thought the Cong had flooded the market with cheap heroin and marijuana and opium. I told him that if you could follow the people who sold the drugs to the GIs, you'd probably find the Cong. It's the dark ages.

"It's okay," Hammurabi confided, "we all know you're the resident political analyst and malcontent. I was just wondering if they'd ever considered it. They've just about considered every fucking thing else. Talk about the dark ages. Man, what a time warp."

I sat back against the retaining wall, trying to relax. But I couldn't keep still. My nose and my ears felt like they were crawling all over my face. I had to keep checking to make sure they were still in place. Patterns appeared in the pitch-black sky. They kept moving, changing design and colors. I knew I wasn't going to do anyone much good if we got hit and it started bugging me that maybe this wasn't such a good idea. Tripping in the 'Nam. Patterns drew into the shape of dead Cong turning black in the sun. They were on display for the local citizenry. "See?" the bodies said. "This is what happens if you're a Cong and you get your ticket stamped." Dead GIs pulled out of mud holes, dead for days. "See?" I tried seeing Japanese flower arrangements. But the images only lasted for seconds before turning into decapitations. They were the heads of Chinese mercenaries that had been taken in the valley. My nose felt like it was somewhere down by my throat and my ears kept crawling over the top of my head. They met on top, where they carried on a conversation.

"Sure is quiet," one ear said.

"Don't you hear them?" the other ear said.

"Who? What?"

"Them. They're breathing."

"Who?"

"The Cong. They collect ears, you know."

I touched my ears, made them stop talking. How do I explain this to the sergeant of the guard? I was worried about myself. I began to worry about Hammurabi and Young. They were quiet and deeply involved in their own trips.

"You guys handling all of this?" I asked.

"This acid's heavy, man," Hammurabi replied.

"It's okay, you guys," Young broke in. "I've done this stuff twice before and I'm a little used to it. You'll be all right."

"Yeah, but you did it back in Australia, not here," Hammurabi detailed for Young.

"Well," Young went on, "as far as I can tell we haven't quite peaked, yet, but were getting there fast. If it gets too heavy, try to at least remember that you're on acid. Heavy tripping starts when you forget what's influencing you. That's why I didn't want to do this alone. When you're on the edge of human experience, it's good to have friends along."

"The edge of human experience?" I asked.

"Dig it, Trevor. This isn't your common, everyday turn of events. It's an experiment, don't you think?" Young asked.

I began to wonder about all of it. Young had been described as a maniac and lunatic by the battery commander and a few others. I maintained that the battery commander was a maniac, along with the rest of us, excluding me. Now, I had doubts about myself. Hippie rhetoric, back in the World, espoused drug experimentation and the exploration of the inner universe. What we saw in the stars was no more vast or inexplicable than what lived in our minds and spirits. Drugs served as a spaceship that took you inside yourself. Forgetting that you took the drug was like a spaceship that's lost contact with earth. It was dangerous. But it was also where real exploration began. I had my doubts about losing contact in a combat zone that had been hot and seemed to be getting hotter. Was tripping on acid in a combat zone a valid exploration into all that is human, or is it insanity? I didn't know. I had learned already that living the way I did created a space and a time where morality and immorality touched. Guys went back to the World after a year of surviving in the bush. They thought that nothing could kill them. They had survived and now the rest of time was theirs. They had dared death and won, so they behaved that way back in the World. God, I thought, if I ever get back to the World, what am I going to be? I wrenched myself free from my wondering thoughts. Brought myself back to the guard bunker, facing the pitch-black night.

I wanted to do something, not just sit quietly thinking about the exploration of the unknown. I bumped the ammunition can that contained some hand flares.

"I'm gonna shoot off a white cluster," I told Hammurabi and Young, "just for something to do. My eyes need something real to look at."

"Are you hallucinating?" Young asked.

"Fuck yes, aren't you?" I told him.

"Dig it, man," Young replied.

"There it is," Hammurabi added.

I prepared the flare, leaned out from under the overhang and slammed the butt plate on a sandbag. It detonated loudly, with the sound of screeching air screaming in my psychedelic ears. It left a luminous smoke trail arching up and away from our bunker. In three seconds, it exploded into five small chunks of ignited white phosphorus. They fell gracefully, burning brightly for a few seconds, lighting up half an acre of Vietnam beneath. The smell of burned powder put my nose back in its place. The noise disciplined my ears.

But there was hardly anything to see. There wasn't supposed to be anything there to see. The noise and the light and the smell, all of these were drawn away quickly, snuffed out by the Vietnamese night. It's a normal thing to shoot off hand flares. No one thinks much about it. You do it, or someone else does it, and then it's over.

We, however, were aghast. Our perceptions weren't normal. The sound was intense and so altered and animated that it seemed as if I had released a life from within the flare tube. The tube contained a brief and concentrated existence that, when released, raced out of the tube, opened its eyes, saw a fraction of life. And then, is that all there is? It faded out, dying, leaving light vapors for our psychedelic eyes to view. The hood of night shrouded us over again and the patterns inside my eyes danced and transformed with unending, syncopated, aboriginal rhythms. This, I knew, was peaking. I wanted to shoot off all the flares and at the same time I knew I shouldn't. I would not. They were no more than stupid little orgasms.

"The sound and the fury," I said.

"Signifying nothing," Young replied.

"What?" Hammurabi asked.

"Shakespeare, "I explained.

"And Faulkner," Young qualified.

"Oh," Hammurabi sighed.

Young leaned back, stretched his legs. "God, this is in-fucking credible. I'm shaking all over. I feel like my hands and my feet are back in the World or something. I can't feel them."

"I know, I know," Hammurabi agreed, "My eyeballs feel like they're outside, looking in on me. I think I'm scared."

"You're supposed to be scared, Ham. You're on acid. This is a trip through a wild quadrant in space and time. I'm scared too. Are you scared, Leon?"

"There it is, man, there it is."

My mind was uncoiling. I felt like my spirit was on a long vacation, leaving the rest of me behind. It was so dark. What was going on down in the valley? I wanted to shoot the machine gun into the valley but knew I wouldn't. I hated the machine gun. I hated it because others loved it. Others still claimed it was nothing more than an instrument. And war is nothing but violence. So what? Fear is a thing. You can find it in the bottom of your guts. Fear and double fear.

"What time?" I asked.

I saw Young's radium coated dial float up.

"Quarter to one."

"Do you think it will happen?" Hammurabi wanted to know.

We all knew what he meant, and we were waiting for it. The Cong struck at one o'clock. 0100 hours. You could set your watch by it. Why do they always hit us at one? I asked myself. They don't, I answered, not always, just usually. People were moving around up on the firebase. Howitzers were shifting, oiled metal breech blocks sliding through oiled metal channels.

"They've been warming things up a bit," Hammurabi confided. "Every time they do it, they throw in more rounds, and bigger."

"It's a ploy," Young explained, "a diversion. They don't want the hill. They want Dalat."

"They can't take Dalat without the hill, Leon," Hammurabi went on. He sighed. "They need this fucking hill," he whispered.

"And they're coming tonight for it?" I asked.

"No, Trevor," Hammurabi told me, "but maybe for us?"

I shuddered. I didn't want to hear it. The Cong had our range bracketed with cunning and appalling accuracy. Every night they threw incoming at us they hit the bunker with the artillery computer in it, FDC. They had stamped a few of our tickets as well. But nothing permanent, so far. Hammurabi only voiced a common concern.

"Let it happen, Ham," I said, "we're dug in. They can't overrun us. It's cat and mouse. They're trying to psych us out. Why else would they always start up at one o'clock? But I bet if they could get inside your mind right now, or Leon's or mine right now, they'd freak out. They're bastards trying to psych us out. But they can't."

"'cause we're already psyched out," Young added.

"There is it."

No one bothered to check the time. It must have been one o-clock because, down in the valley, where I had been gazing in the star-light scope, one red streak, then another, and one more licked out in silence and were gone. They were mortar rounds heading our way. Our bunker and two others faced in that direction, and we all opened up, shooting tracer rounds toward the streaks. The Duster and the Quad-50s followed our lead. Then we took two rockets from the ruins of the mansion. Guns three and four fired high explosive and beehive rounds into the heap of rubble. Another howitzer fired illumination rounds over the valley and the night came alive. From close in we took small arms fire.

Hammurabi was working the machine gun and I fed it. Young began working out with the grenade launcher, firing methodically at the source of the small arms fire. It didn't make sense, we realized later. The AK rounds were too far away. Who were they shooting at? More rounds came in on us and we knew they were going for FDC, or perhaps the guns and ammunition. It was the same routine as before and we knew the results even before they were in. The incoming stopped and so did we. There wasn't anyone down in the valley to shoot at. Fear receded. It was over for a while, unless it wasn't. They say fear is squelched by anger, but we were too freaked out to be angry.

The bunker smelled of spent powder and fried nerves. What was next? It grew deadly quiet all over the firebase. The sergeant of the guard came by for a casualty check.

"Everything all right down there?" he asked.

"Sure, no sweat," I told him.

"It' fine, sergeant," Young replied.

"Okay, sergeant," Hammurabi said.

"Is that you Ham?" the sergeant asked.

"Yeah."

"Good. Stay there tonight." He walked off to see about the rest.

We sat quietly for I don't know how long, maybe an hour. All I could see was the ugly chain of mortar rounds exploding over the firebase as they hit in the trees or the B-40 wire around FDC. I could see shrapnel in them. In the morning someone would investigate and we all knew what would be find. In the valley they would find jury-rigged mortar tubes, aimed and preset to go off at 0100 hours. In the ruins they'd find the rockets worked in the same way. It was a psych job straight out of the Cong book of guerrilla tactics.

"Is this what God has in mind?" Young asked.

No one answered. Was he enticing us into another one of his theological discussions? I didn't care what his motives were. I wanted to talk so I wouldn't dwell on the tactics of the Viet Cong.

"What do you mean?" I asked him.

"What I'm getting at, you guys, is that maybe we can change our karma. I mean, who else can change it?"

"The draft board," I suggested.

"Right on, Trevor," Hammurabi concurred.

"That's bullshit, you guys." Young went on. "No one can actually force you to be drafted. We all allowed it. We did not will it to be different. Maybe the law strongly stated that you had to fight, but, like they say, the final choice is always the individual's private decision."

"Who says that, Leon?" Hammurabi wanted to know.

"Anyone who believes in karma. You might think that karma is another word for predestination, but I think that the choices that you make change your karma. It provides for a totally different set of choices you can make for the future."

"Wasn't it your karma to come here, Leon?" I asked.

"Yeah, and I'm trying to change it. That's why I'm doing this acid. I don't really know what LSD is, except that those who do it have a different karma than those who never have."

"Everyone's karma is different, Leon," Hammurabi suggested.

"There it is, Ham, but I feel that if you take acid, you somehow make a choice about your karma. It's a conscious choice to humble yourself, to admit that reason and perception and logic are, at the most, three dimensional, and explain virtually nothing of real importance or lasting value. I mean, people get all tight-assed about money and goods and technology. They think those things are a true measure of what's important in life. But the spirituality in man is where it's at and we'll never find it in a telescope or get there in a car or make it in a steel mill. We have to be humble."

"And taking acid's humble?" I asked.

"It can and should be, you guys. I don't take it for entertainment. Do you think this is entertaining? Is worrying about the next funking mortar round that might land on your head entertaining? Fuck no! But this war doesn't have jack shit to do with LSD. This war's our karma. I think acid's just a way to change your karma. But you have to have the right frame of mind. You have to think about it and prepare. Even then, it can only help you help yourself."

"Leon! For God's sake, man," Hammurabi interrupted. "We could just as easily have got our ass blown away. Don't you care? I mean, somebody out there wants us dead and they don't give a shit about karma. Fuck! Here you are rapping to us about how acid's a key to the universe, but if you don't relate to what's happening here and now, we might be getting our brains splattered all over the inside of this god damn bunker. Can you dig it, man?"

I could see that Young was looking over at me, wanting me to help settle down Hammurabi. We both knew what was going on inside him. Sebeok and Wilkins and Crick. They were all friends of his who had had their brains splattered all over the inside of a bunker just a few minutes after Hammurabi had left.

"It's all right, Ham. I guess we'll make it through the night. Sebeok and Wilkins and Crick had their own karma, and you have yours. I don't think LSD's the key to the universe, Ham, 'cause the magic's in us, not the drug."

"Why take it then?" Hammurabi pouted.

Young spoke again. "Probably you shouldn't take it very often. Most people never will take it. That doesn't mean they can never be their own karma. I only think you should take it to be humble and realize you aren't really in control anyway, so why not cool it?

"I think that if everyone in the fucking army, I mean ours and theirs and everyone else's, took acid just once, if that happened, I bet everyone would just walk away from war and go do something peaceful and productive."

"It won't happen, Leon. Never."

"I know, so that's why I'm doing it now. And I think you guys are doing it for the same reason, even if you don't know it."

"What reason?" I asked.

"To experiment with your own karma. It's like rolling the spiritual dice."

"What if you lose?" I wondered.

"Then you're out of the game. But there's always another game."

"Reincarnation?" Hammurabi asked.

"There it is."

"And if you win?" I asked.

"I don't know, Trevor. I guess I could say something like eternal life, except how can life be anything but eternal?"

"You can always die, Leon. Otherwise, there wouldn't be war. Otherwise, generals wouldn't be possessed by the devil, and privates too, only generals more."

"All I can say, Ham," Young responded, "is that maybe their souls, their spirits will be released on the day there's no more wars."

"How would you like it if you were dead?" Hammurabi wanted to know.

"I'm not afraid of death, I don't think," Young answered. "It's the dying part that bugs me. Even more than that, it's the pain that may come with it."

"Violent death, "I had to say, "is hell. What are the last thoughts of someone who has died violently? Can you read it in their eyes?"

"Maybe." Hammurabi answered. "If they have a head left."

"It seems like you want me to have all the answers, Ham, or you want me to predict the future. I can't. All I want to do is change my karma. I'm thinking about my future, my spiritual future. All I want to do is get out from under this war, one way or another, 'cause it's bad karma, for all of us. I don't know if LSD's the way, but I know being what the World wants us to be sure as hell isn't."

The World, it seems, has changed its mind about what it wanted from us, or maybe it never really knew. All I know is that I thought differently after that night. Nothing bad happened to us that night. Something good came out of it; it's called a memory about making a statement. I was doing something to change my karma if there is such a thing. Young and Hammurabi finished their tours and rejoined the World. Like me, they probably married and maybe have a family and are doing okay. Sometimes I think I'd like to know what Leon Young really thinks about karma now. Was Young able to change his karma and does he think his karma is good now? Does he believe in LSD, that it makes you humble, that it can help you change your karma? I don't know about any of that. When I came back to the World, I gave up my liberal arts education. Today I'm a CPA. Mine is an ipso facto computer world. And I have no time to contemplate my karma, except money wise. In that sense, my karma is wonderful. I wonder what Young dreams about. My doctor gives me pills to keep my dreams away. But sometimes the dreams overpower the medicine, or I forget to take it. Then this is what I dream: Reincarnation.

hill 1503

you scan the château in your star-light scope
the green vapor drifts among the ruins
like a dragon searching for ancestral ghosts
you stand at the crossroads and make your choice
so many times you said no, when all along it was yes
now your choice hangs in the moonlight
seen through the web of a dream catcher
now you hear the hollow ring of a mortar tube
your sacrament lost in the snick of your lock-and-load
now you feel the recoil,
and in your pocket, one trillion seashells measure out
your share
one shell at a time
one rhythm, one rhyme
one poem, one line

the moon's koan

once she filled your arms with her warm and tender body
once she filled your heart with her artless love
now she dwells in a world you cannot know
her eyes, shadowed in the moonlight
standing in the water, watching you
a blue sky, unseen in the blue sky
rocket grenades hit your convoy
you don't know the one lying dead in the road
turning black and starting to bloat
you don't know the one bleeding red
but some mother knows that Cong lying dead
tonight, women will sing the moon's koan
and write his name in stone

I t was late and Henry Browning was about to enter his one long dream. But then the phone rang.

"Yes?"

"That you, Henry?"

"Yes, it's me. David?"

"Yeah. Sorry to bug you so late but I just got done with an advocacy case that I think you'd be interested in."

"Come on over then. I'll get up."

Henry hung up. He looked over at his wife. She watched him sleepily, curled up on her side in the dark. He pulled himself out of bed, put on a pair of jeans, a sweatshirt and some moccasins.

"It's okay, Helen," he advised. "David's coming over. We'll stay in the kitchen. Go back to sleep."

Helen mumbled, held out her hand to touch her husband, then fell back to sleep.

Henry thought about David as he washed his face and brushed his teeth. Well, I guess he was working late again, like always. That program would fold if it weren't for him and I'm glad he's the director.

David was a psychologist working with Vietnam veterans. His work generally referred him to veterans with police records. Henry met him in court while Henry was trying to defend a Vietnam veteran. The veteran had stolen a police cruiser and hidden it in the woods. It was still lost. The veteran was still in jail and David was trying to find the cruiser. Henry's practice specialized in Vietnam veteran cases. Through the years Henry and David grew to be close friends. They were both Vietnam veterans. Henry a lawyer and David a psychologist. They were making it in the free market society. They were solid citizens who believed that by helping others you helped yourself. Sometimes Henry and David would talk about their dreams because they were friends and trusted one another. Also, their wives, Helen and Alice, suggested that they do so, and Henry and David tended to listen to their wives for they were both intelligent and loving. It was therapy, they said, to talk about your dreams. "Some dreams." Henry and David always seemed to add.

Henry made some coffee and waited in the kitchen. Helen's current favorite novel sat on the table. It was "Sirens of Titan," by Kurt Vonnegut, Jr. Henry had read it once, in Vietnam, and then twice more when he came home. And now Helen was reading it again and again. It was, among other things, about the veterans of a useless war. Car lights announced David's arrival just as the coffee perked up, just as Henry finished the first chapter.

A gentle knock and a quiet unlatching of the front door and David stood in the hall, smiling as always, short and muscular and bald at thirty-five. Henry took his coat and hat, put them in the vestibule closet along with Helen and Henry's coats and hats.

"It's been a long day, Henry. I had an advocacy case in San Diego that ran from four this morning until now. The DA's on my advocacy board so he let me in on it."

"I can imagine so, David. Care for some coffee?" Henry directed him into the kitchen. They always did their best talking in the Browning kitchen. At David and Alice's, they did their best talking in Paul's bedroom. Paul was their son.

They sat down to some coffee. Henry made cookies that day and he put them out, too. They didn't taste very good, though. Henry accidentally added onion powder where the recipe had asked for baking powder.

"So, what's up, David?"

David leaned back. "Oh man, I've been with this lost soul named Zorro Two all day long. He's in the county slammer in San Diego waiting for arraignment tomorrow on two counts of murder."

"Murder what?"

"Don't know. Probably not in the first."

"Let's hear it. If that's what you want to talk about."

"Yeah, that's it, all right. Last night I got a call in the middle of the night from Karfeldt, that new Assistant DA. Anyway, they have this Zorro Two fellow down there and he's flipping out and Karfeldt wants me to help them out. They guy's a Vietnam veteran, it seems, and maybe he'd settle down some if another veteran was there."

David finished his coffee and Henry poured him some more.

"'I want to help.' I tell Karfeldt. When I got there, I convinced them to let me talk to the guy in the visitor chamber so we can talk. Well, it turns out that Zorro Two's quite in control of himself if you can relax in front of him. I was calm so he was too. They let me bring in a recorder because of the research I'm doing. I want you to hear it.'"

Henry nodded and David pushed the play button.

"Is this thing on? My name is Zorro Two. I live in Hell's Valley outside of Escondido. Yesterday I killed two punks and so now I'm in jail."

David asked him if he could figure out why he did it.

"'Cause they were punks."

David asked him what happened.

"Yesterday I left my girlfriend's house after a nap on her couch. I . . . I had a bad dream, and I didn't want to be alone. My girlfriend . . . she works, so I was there lone. I went down to this nice little bar where I know the owners. They're nice. It's a nice place. Got plants in the windows and sunlight and good music on the juke.

"I was just sitting there having a coke when these two punks came in and sat across the bar from me. They're a little bit drunk and you can see they were really looking to hang one on and get obnoxious and obscene and just real mean. You know?"

David said he thought he did.

"Anyway, they kept ordering drinks and talking real dirty and mean, just to talk dirty and mean. They wanted attention and were such punks they didn't know how to get it 'cept by talking dirty. I try not to hate people, but I knew I hated them.

"Finally, the bar maid asks them to leave, and they said they wanted more drinks. She calls the manager, and he tells them leave or he'll call the Man. I was really sick of their faces, but I kept quiet 'cause I know the owners and they try to run a decent place. These fuckers didn't have any respect."

The tape ran on wordlessly for a time. Henry and David exchanged glances.

"The punks got up and left. I followed them. They stopped on the sidewalk outside. I guess they were wondering what to do next. I came up behind them and said, 'Hey, man!' And they turned to face me. Then I cuffed the biggest one in the face real hard. And right away I turn and run down the alley. I wanted them to chase me, and they did. I had my Harley parked back there in a little parking lot. No one was around. They were yelling and swearing, and I let them almost catch me.

"Then I turned on them and did an extended squat thrust with both fists into the solar plexus of the big guy. He buckled over real easy and before he was down I did a three-sixty round kick to the chin of the other punk. By then the big guy was up again and he had his blade out."

It got quiet on the tape again. Jail sounds registered in the background.

"I was carrying a scalpel. My girlfriend's a nurse," Zorro Two explained to the recorder. "Before he could move on me I had him sliced open from gut to throat. The other guy took one look at his buddy's guts spilling out on the parking lot and he took off back up the alley. I got on my Harley and caught up to him. I speed shifted into second gear. The front wheel came off the ground and hit him square in the back. I could feel his back breaking. Then the back wheel ran over him."

Henry whistled softly, shook his head. On the tape, Zorro Two cleared his throat once more.

"I didn't know what to do. It all happened before I had a chance to think about it. I was in a strange mood before it happened. But they were punks. I'm not sorry I did it. I know I have to be punished 'cause that's the law. But I don't think I'll ever be sorry, except maybe in front of God."

David asked what happened then.

"Well, I didn't know what to do. All I knew was that I was on my machine, so I headed for Tijuana. Somebody must have seen what went on in the parking lot 'cause by the time I reached the boarder there were about a hundred cops who jammed me up, pointing everything they had at me."

David pushed the stop button, took off his glasses and placed them on the table. The refrigerator came on, hummed for a minute, then left them quieter than before.

"I turned off the tape at that point because," David explained, "that's what I do."

Henry knew.

"Zorro Two asked me who I was. He didn't remember the introduction. I reminded him that I had been called in to talk to him, that I was a Vietnam veteran. He asked me how anyone knew that he was a 'Nam vet. 'Your girlfriend told us,' I said. We talked about Vietnam for hours after that, back in his cell. He told me he was self-educated and that he read everything that he could. He was really interested in philosophy, especially Voltaire. In 'Nam his Zippo lighter had the name Pangloss written on it."

"Who's that?" Henry asked.

"That's the dude who keeps saying this is the best of all possible worlds. It's in a book called Candide, by Voltaire."

"Oh."

"I asked him if he thought this was the best of all possible worlds. He said he doubted it. Too many conflicting philosophies, like Vietnam. He used to get medals for killing people he didn't know, who, in other circumstances, may have been friends. He killed everyone like he killed those punks. In cold blood. And everyone congratulated him. They told him everything was cool, even if he felt sort of bad about it, because the philosophy that went into it was bigger than the individual. Anyway, they said, the ultimate responsibility belongs to society, so don't worry."

David pulled over another kitchen chair and propped up his legs.

"Zorro Two said that nobody told him about the dreams, no one said what it'd be like ten year later. Society changes, he said."

"How long's this Zorro Two been back home? By the way, what the hell kind of name is Zorro Two?" Henry asked.

"Don't know about the name. I forgot to ask. He's been home for about thirteen years. Special Forces pulling special operations when he was in 'Nam. Real primordial stuff. He's a classic case of no one bothering to deactivate him. I'm amazed he hung around for thirteen years before acting out."

"Some guys seem to get over it," Henry suggested.

"It's a good thing that they do, Henry. Zorro Two, I'm afraid, didn't. Yesterday he acted something out. A victim of his own circumstances?"

"He's captain of his own ship, whether he wants to be or not."

"Henry, you're such an asshole sometimes."

"I know, I know. It's the devil's advocate in me, I guess."

"Maybe Zorro Two believes in being his own captain, in a way. There was method to his madness. I mean, at least he took out some real punks."

"Were they, David?"

"Yeah. Karfeldt ran a check on them. Zorro Two had them pegged, all right. Karlfeldt was tickled pink, figured Zorro Two saved the taxpayers a lot of money when he offed those two. I'm confused on this on, Henry."

Henry could see that.

"After thirteen years of delayed stress," David went on, "he finally pulls the pin. He commits an anti-social act. But not blindly. It was directed toward people who he felt deserved to die."

"Lots of people probably deserve to die, David, but Zorro Two can't just go around killing them."

"Henry? Don't be stupid. You and I and Zorro Two and countless other people went around killing people for less of a reason than being punks. They gave us medals for doing it."

"David? You sound as if you're condoning what he did."

"No. I'm trying to put things in perspective, that's all."

David helped himself to more coffee, offered the pot to Henry.

"You know what Zorro Two really wants, or at least what he told me he wants?"

Henry wanted to know.

"He wants to be tried for murder, but not yesterday's murder. He wants to go back thirteen years and be tried for those murders instead."

Henry remembered several occasions when that possibility had been discussed between David and himself. He asked himself why David was here tonight. What was it about this case that had them up in the middle of a weeknight?

David tried one of Henry's cookies, made a sour face as he chewed it.

"You make these?"

"They didn't turn out so well. Sorry. The dog likes 'em though." Henry reached under the table with the rest of David's cookie. The dog, an old golden retriever, sniffed it, then took it softly.

It was quiet again, except for the dog's chewing noises. Henry collected his thoughts. Henry and David both felt sad about the war, about being in the war. But they were living with it. They were coping. Or were they? Was sitting up all night in the kitchen talking about the war really coping? Maybe they were using Zorro Two as the subject, but the object of the whole thing, Henry realized over and over, was to subjugate their own syndrome.

"Do you know why this case is different?" David asked.

The more it's different, the more it's the same, Henry mused.

"The reason for it being different is the reason you're here. Right, David?"

"Yes. Zorro Two started asking me all sorts of questions about 'Nam. Where, when, why? You know. After a while I felt I could ask him what I really wanted to know. I asked, 'What did 'Nam have to do with you killing those two guys?'"

David took a long breath.

"If you go back to the tape, you'll hear that Zorro Two said he was taking a nap and had a bad dream."

Henry sat forward. The chair was uncomfortable.

"It's an odd dream, Henry. Want to know why?"

Henry feared that he already knew why.

"Zorro Two's dream is a recurring dream. That's why it's part of a nightmare. Somewhere, way back in the subconscious interior, Zorro Two's nightmare holds together. It never falls away. Another part of why it's a nightmare is because he's wishing, in the dream, that he was only dreaming."

Henry forced himself to ask what the dream was.

"It's returning to Vietnam. It's going back."

This was the same dream that Henry and David wondered about a dozen times. They both had the dream three or four times a year. Now, someone else was sharing their dream. How many others?

"What frightens me," David went on, "is that after he had that dream the last time, he pulled the pin on his emotions."

"Are you equating the two, David?"

"It's the nature of the dream that has to be equated to the nature of the act."

"How?"

"Wouldn't you agree that that dream, for Zorro Two, and for you and me, is a symbol? And that that symbol is the preemption of the will?"

"Maybe. I don't know, David, and neither do you. It's a terrible dream for me because it's one that I'm standing outside of. I know how it ends but it's so real that I can't imagine it's a dream. Until I wake up. And when I do wake up, I feel like Zorro Two did yesterday. I hate. That preemption of will rolls right into my consciousness because I don't will myself to hate. I just do."

"You hate yourself, Henry."

Henry nodded.

"But it's not just hate because there's fear as well. There's fear because, like you said, you know how the dream ends. Part of the fear derives from the dream being so fucking real. It's so strong that it obliterates the power to imagine something other than the dream. It is reality. And the reality is that when you go back this time, you know you're going to die. You're going to die because you didn't die last time."

"And Zorro Two dreams that, too?" Henry asked.

"I think a lot of guys do, some more intensely than others."

"It's just a dream. I can't defend Zorro Two or anybody else because of bad dreams."

"I don't expect you to, Henry, and I didn't bring this over to discuss legal aspects. Zorro Two wants to be found guilty of murder so that when the dream finally overpowers him …"

David didn't know how to finish. He walked into the bathroom, shut the door behind him. Henry sat thinking. Would there ever be a day when in which he didn't sit back and think about Vietnam? Was he really guilty of anything? David confessed once that these flashbacks and dreams and the lingering delinquency of many Vietnam veterans, including himself, were manifestations of the spoiled products of a consumer-oriented society. But Henry had pointed out that not everyone who suffered ill-effects from the war was spoiled. Take the Blacks, for instance, he suggested. They had, per capita, taken on a heavier burden from the onset, and were they now being considered spoiled?

David returned. "Poor Zorro Two." He said, "What will happen to him? We're supposed to know. We're the decision makers. We tell society what to do with guys like Zorro Two. But I'm damned if I know what to do. But there's something going on inside Zorro Two that's a least a start, I think. Something we can learn from."

"What's that, David?"

"Deep down inside he seemed at least to make a distinction between punks and non-punks. I don't think he picked that up from his reading or even anything he learned. It was just instinct."

"Instinct is where it's at, David?"

"Yeah, maybe. Instinct wakes us up from the nightmares."

"But the last time Zorro Two woke up from a nightmare he killed two people. Was that an example of instinct?"

"No, Henry, it was instinct that told him they were punks, though."

"I think you are condoning what he did. Are you, David?"

"No. I'm a professional. I . . ."

"Don't give me that nonsense, David. So what if you're a professional. You still have an opinion. And I think you agree with Zorro Two's behavior because . . ."

"Because it's a way of not having nightmares?" David raised his voice. "Yeah, maybe you're right." He paced the room, breathing heavily, working his fingers into fists. "Sometimes I can't help what I think, man. Can you dig it? Maybe I do condone it. Maybe I do wish I had enough guts to take out a few punks before I—before I die in my fucking sleep!"

David cried. Henry hugged him, let him know he was there, that he cared. Another night. Another little damn broken. Where did all the water go? It's all headed back. Helen, who had heard the conversation drifting in and out of her own dreams, and who knew, instinctively, about flashbacks and nightmares, came downstairs. She fixed soup, homemade chicken noodle soup. For all of them. This, too, was a recurring scene. Sometimes David's wife would fix soup for Henry when Henry needed David's help. Or David would fix soup for Helen, then Henry for Alice. Talking over coffee and homemade soup. It never really cured anything. It just kept Henry and David, in their dreams, from going back for good.

the choice

find their names
find their tags
find their boots still caked in mud
leave something for the living
take something from the dead
stand in solemn silence
long before it started,
that's when you made you choice
and now,
when you feel the recoil of you rifle
now you know,
your choice was not to fight
but to surrender

dogs

in the 'Nam, the locals don't name their dogs
in the 'Nam, dogs die of distemper, or get eaten
but you rescue them when you can
because saving dogs and giving them names is like home
but when you go home
the dogs stay here, and forget their names

the one thing

you say that going to the 'Nam
was the one thing you should have done
that if you had it to do over, this time you'd go
not to see it in their eyes
or to partake in the chaos
but that's surely what you would remember
after you do the one thing you should have done

all day

you board the plane,
you pull down the canvas seat and strap in,
the man across from you has long hair,
he wears a gray t-shirt and blue jeans,
you wear a thousand-yard stare,
he watches you,
and when you watch back, he looks away
the engines turn over and catch
you creep forward and gain speed
you lift off the tarmac, rotate, and bank hard over Ban
Mê Thuột,
you know what lies beyond
not the terraced hillsides
not the switchbacks on Highway Eleven
or the Na River glinting in the sun,
the man asks how long you've been here,
you say all day
some of you goes home
some of you stays in the 'Nam
some of you waits until last 'Nam vet left standing,
is you

your own self

you say it's not the gun that kills them all
not the bullet, or the frag
not the Claymore mine, or the high explosive round
not the napalm, or death by burning
but it's you
it's you who's in charge of your own self

some of you

some of you goes home
some of you stays in the 'Nam
and some of you waits
waits until every 'Nam vet but you, is gone
until you're the last one
the last one to think it
to say it or to write it
the very last,
until in the blue jungle, there rings a tiny bell.

the ARVN

the Army of the Republic of Vietnam,
some of them are like you,
whose only motive is to remain in one piece,
except they're never in one piece
you watch two ARVN boys in the market,
brothers or cousins, or maybe just friends,
they stand close, holding hands, not talking, not smiling,
and then you understand,
they are saying goodbye
maybe forever
tonight women sing the moon's koan
and write the names in stone

the White Elephant Division

you call them the Montagnards,
but they're known as the White Elephant Division,
you give them small arms,
you give them mountain howitzers and train them how
to fight,
but for them there is no South Vietnam, and no North
Vietnam,
they make no distinction between warring factions,
they kill them all, and let you sort them out

the last vestige of Sun Yat-Sen

you age in the 'Nam, but not like the Viet Dan
who carry dated weapons, who's uniforms are faded and
patched,
they gather around their cooking fires,
the gray ones, standing in the monsoon rain, waiting to
move on,
they are the Kuomintang, the last vestige of Sun Yat-Sen

China White

your stomach turns,
your bones ache, and it hurts to move,
way past time for another fix,
but you're broke, except for the beggar's coin,
that silver dollar you carry for good luck here in the
'Nam
sell it for five bucks, MPC,
buy your next vial of China White,
there, it don't mean nuthin'

universal soldier

you say it's not your gun that kills,
not your bullet, or frag, or Claymore mine,
not your high explosive round, or the napalm,
but it's you who made the choice,
for you are the universal soldier
there it is

About Lee Henschel Jr.

Lee Henschel Jr. was born in Minneapolis, Minnesota, and began his writing life when he was twelve. He is the author of three previous volumes of *The Sailing Master* saga: *Book One, Coming of Age, Book Two, The Long Passage,* and *Book Three: Letter of Marque*. Lee's poems and short stories have been published in numerous literary journals and anthologies, including *Lost Lake Folk Opera,* where "The 'Nam" first appeared in the April 2015, Black April issue marking the fortieth anniversary of the Fall of Saigon. His collection, *Short Stories of Vietnam,* was published in 1981.

"Each day I give thanks for any writing talent I've been given, and I vow to honor the gift, to nurture it, and to share it."

—Lee Henschel Jr.